CHERRY AMES, COMPANION NURSE

CHERRY AMES COMPANION NURSE

By

HELEN WELLS

SPRINGER PUBLISHING COMPANY

New York

Springer Publishing Company, LLC
11 West 42nd Street
New York, NY 10036-8002
www.springerpub.com

Acquisitions Editor: Sally J. Barhydt
Series Editor: Harriet S. Forman
Production Editor: Carol Cain
Cover design: Mimi Flow
Composition: Apex Publishing, LLC

08   09   10   11/   5   4   3   2   1

Library of Congress Cataloging-in-Publication Data

Wells, Helen, 1910–
  [Cherry Ames, companion nurse]
  Companion nurse / by Helen Wells.
      p. cm. — (Cherry Ames nurse stories)
  Summary: Cherry enjoys traveling through Great Britain as a private nurse for
historical novelist Martha Logan, but the museums they visit are plagued by a
perplexing series of art thefts.
  ISBN-13: 978-0-8261-0431-1 (alk. paper)
  ISBN-10: 0-8261-0431-2 (alk. paper)
 [1. Nurses—Fiction. 2. Art thefts—Fiction. 3. Art museums—Fiction.
4. Museums—Fiction. 5. Great Britain—History—Elizabeth II, 1952—Fiction.
6. Mystery and detective stories.]   I. Title.
  PZ7.W4644Cdd 2007
  [Fic]—dc22
                                                      2007035485

Printed in the United States of America by Bang Printing

Contents

Foreword

~~~~~~

Helen Wells, the author of the Cherry Ames stories, said, "I've always thought of nursing, and perhaps you have, too, as just about the most exciting, important, and rewarding profession there is. Can you think of any other skill that is *always* needed by everybody, everywhere?"

I was and still am a fan of Cherry Ames. Her courageous dedication to her patients; her exciting escapades; her thirst for knowledge; her intelligent application of her nursing skills; and the respect she achieved as a registered nurse (RN) all made it clear to me that I was going to follow in her footsteps and become a nurse—nothing else would do.

Thousands of other young readers were motivated by Cherry Ames to become RNs as well. Through her thought-provoking stories, Cherry Ames led a steady stream of students into schools of nursing across the country well into the 1960s and 1970s when the series ended.

Readers who remember enjoying these books in the past will take pleasure in reading them again now—whether or not they chose nursing as their life's work. Perhaps they will share them with others and even motivate a person or two to choose nursing as their career.

My nursing path has been rich and satisfying. I have delivered babies, cared for people in hospitals and in their homes, and saved lives. I have worked at the bedside and served as an administrator, I have published journals, written articles, taught students, consulted, and given expert testimony. Never once did I regret my decision to become a nurse.

During the time I was publishing a nursing journal, I became acquainted with Robert Wells, brother of Helen Wells. In the course of conversation I learned that Ms. Wells had passed on and left the Cherry Ames copyright to Mr. Wells. Because there is a shortage of nurses here in the US today, I thought, "Why not bring Cherry back to motivate a whole new generation of young people? Why not ask Mr. Wells for the copyright to Cherry Ames?" Mr. Wells agreed, and the republished series is dedicated both to Helen Wells, the original author, and to her brother, Robert Wells, who transferred the rights to me. I am proud to ensure the continuation of Cherry Ames into the twenty-first century.

The final dedication is to you, both new and former readers of Cherry Ames: It is my dream that you enjoy Cherry's nursing skills as well as her escapades. I hope that young readers will feel motivated to choose nursing as their life's work. Remember, as Helen Wells herself said: there's no other skill that's "*always* needed by everybody, everywhere."

Harriet Schulman Forman, RN, EdD
Series Editor

CHERRY AMES, COMPANION NURSE

CHAPTER I

Spencer Club Reunion

"COME IN, CHERRY!" BERTHA UNLOCKED AND SWUNG open the door to the Spencer Club's apartment.

"Cherry must go in first," Mai Lee insisted. "She's the guest of honor!"

Josie, reaching out for Cherry's suitcase, said, "I'll take it. You go on in—and welcome back!"

Cherry relinquished the suitcase and bowed. "Fellow nurses, I thank you!" She walked into the small, attractive gold-and-white living room, and laughed when she saw the banner draped across the room. In large, amateurishly printed, red-crayon letters it read:

WELCOME, CHERRY! S.C.'S MOST FAMOUS MEMBER!

"Famous or infamous," Cherry said. "That's a really wonderful welcome! Shall I make a speech of thanks?"

"Just sit down and cool off," said Josie, who put down Cherry's suitcase and sat on it, puffing.

It was hot in the New York apartment at eight o'clock on a Wednesday evening in late August. But it was home in a special sense—this rather cramped Greenwich Village apartment that the Spencer Club nurses shared whenever any or all of them were in New York. Cherry dropped on the sofa and said cheerfully:

"It was even hotter at home in Hilton, Illinois, when I left this afternoon." She mopped her rosy face. "You were dears to come all the way out to the airport to meet me. Oh, I'm so glad to see all of you! But where's Gwen? I thought she'd be home by now."

Mai Lee, a dainty Chinese-American girl, sat down beside Cherry. "Gwen phoned before we left. She's still working, poor dear, on some sort of emergency. You know late hours can't be helped, on private duty—" Mai Lee affectionately squeezed Cherry's hand. "I'm so glad you're here!"

Josie Franklin pushed her glasses up on her forehead and blinked. "Me, too. Only for a fellow Spencer Clubber would I go all the way out to Idlewild."

Bertha Larsen, all smiles, came in from the kitchen carrying a tray with glasses and a pitcher of lemonade. She was a big, hearty farm girl from Minnesota. Bertha passed the cool drinks, saying, "I wish some of our Spencer Club members weren't away just when you're here, Cherry. They'd love to see you."

"I'd like to see them, too," Cherry said. "But then, we're rarely all together at one time." She beamed at her friends and they smiled warmly at Cherry. She was the one who had started the Spencer Club, back in their nursing school days at Spencer Hospital. Her friends called her "our spark plug," adding "Cherry makes things happen." Cherry's high spirits showed in her shining dark eyes, her vivid face, and in the way she tossed back her crisp, dark curls. "How's Vivian?" she asked. "And Ann? And Marie Swift?" They, too, were Cherry's former classmates from nursing school, and Spencer Club members. "How are your jobs?"

Before they could tell her, the telephone rang. Bertha, who answered, reported it was Gwen Jones, still at her job and asking to speak to Cherry.

Cherry went to the telephone. Gwen's excited voice came on.

"Cherry? . . . Hello! There's a special reason why I'm glad you're in New York!"

"What reason? Come on home, Gwen, I'm longing to see you."

"Coming in a minute, but I have to check something with you first. How long is your vacation? Didn't you write us that you have a month? And that you have no definite plans?"

Cherry said, mystified, "That's right. I have some ideas—"

"Well, how would you like to go to England?"

"Wha-a-at?"

"I'll explain when I get there," Gwen said hastily. "Be there in a few minutes. . . . Yes, I said England. G'by," and Gwen hung up.

Cherry repeated the conversation to Bertha, Josie, and Mai Lee. "I think Gwen's out of her mind."

"Well," Mai Lee murmured, "when she phoned for us not to wait supper for her, she did say something about a pretty special sort of emergency."

"What's England got to do with it?" Josie asked.

Placidly, Bertha said they would find out soon. Cherry tried to control her own curiosity. While waiting for Gwen, the other three brought her up to date on Spencer Club news. Marie Swift was on vacation. Vivian Warren was working for a surgeon out West, and loving it. Ann Evans was in Canada with her husband. Bertha reported with enthusiasm on her job as clinic nurse in a settlement house here in New York, near the girls' apartment. Gwen and Josie were on private-duty cases. Mai Lee, now a pediatrician's nurse, said that working with children "is the happiest nursing I ever did.... Cherry, it's your turn to report."

"Yes, how did you like working with the new junior volunteers at Hilton Hospital this past summer?" Mai Lee asked.

"Our teenage Jayvees are a wonderful help at the hospital," Cherry said, "especially in view of the nurse shortage."

The other girls nodded. There simply were not enough nurses to go around. Every nurse had too many patients and worried about having insufficient time to give each patient the fullest attention and care.

"I must admit that helping train the junior volunteers was a load, on top of my job as staff nurse," Cherry said. "I'm really ready for my vacation. England *would* be a wonderful place to spend it."

Mai Lee gave her tinkling laugh. "Look at her! She's all ready to go, at the drop of a hat."

The door flew open and Gwen Jones burst in. "What a day I've had!" she exclaimed. "Where's Cherry?" Gwen's short red hair stood on end and her freckled face was smudged. In other words, she was her usual exuberant self. "Cherry! Hello!" She and Cherry hugged each other. "Hi, kids," Gwen said to the others, and all but bounced down onto the couch. "Have I ever some exciting news to tell you! Gosh, I'm starving—"

Bertha, who was the Spencer Club's best and chief cook, brought in the heaping plateful of homemade potato salad and cold roast beef she had saved for Gwen. Josie solemnly poured her a glass of iced lemonade. Gwen dashed out to wash her hands, then dashed back, sat down, and offered the plate of food to Cherry.

"Have some?" Gwen asked.

"No, thanks. I had dinner on the plane," Cherry said. "What's this about wanting to ship me off to England when I've barely arrived here? A fine welcome! You can't wait to get rid of me!"

Gwen gave her a fond look and said, "Just let me have some nourishment, and I'll tell you all about Martha Logan's broken arm."

"Martha Logan?" Mai Lee repeated. She reached for a book on the coffee table and held it up. It was an historical novel. On the back of the book jacket was a photograph of an attractive woman in sports clothes. "I've been reading this book by Martha Logan. Is the author your patient, Gwen?"

Gwen nodded, gulped down a big bite, and said, "She's the one. By the way, I'm not being unethical in talking to you about my patient, because what happened to Martha Logan probably will be in the newspapers, anyway. She's all set to go to England next week, to do research for her next book, and this afternoon she had a nasty fall. Fell down a whole flight of subway stairs. Broke her arm—her right arm, it's a simple closed fracture—and gashed and bruised both legs, quite badly. She's awfully shaken up, poor thing. *But* she insists on going ahead with her trip."

"Your Dr. Merriam treated her?" Josie asked.

"Yes, he was called by Mrs. Clark, who's one of his long-time private patients. Mrs. Logan and the Clarks are friends," Gwen explained. "She came from the West Coast two or three weeks ago to stay with them before flying to London." Gwen took a long sip of lemonade. "Fortunately, Mrs. Clark was with Martha Logan when she fell. The doctor sent an ambulance to bring her to the hospital. He set her arm there and put on a cast and had her lie down for a while. Mrs. Clark insisted that Martha Logan rest and recover at home rather than at the hospital—thinking of the expense, I guess, and a broken arm really isn't enough reason to occupy a hospital bed."

The other nurses agreed. Gwen paused for breath, then went on, "That's when Dr. Merriam telephoned me. It was five o'clock, and I was just going off duty at Mrs. Jackman's apartment." She turned to Cherry to say, "I'm on private duty, daytime, severe heart case— Well, Doctor asked me to go to the Clarks' apartment and give Martha Logan some comfort measures. Of course I went and did what I could—got her out of her clothes and into a nightgown and into bed, washed her and combed her hair. She was very grateful just for the personal hygiene. I propped her arm on pillows to support it, but we had a hard time finding a comfortable position.

"I let Mrs. Logan rest a while," Gwen went on between bites of her supper, "and then I explained to her that we mustn't let the arm grow stiff. She was awfully game about moving her arm now and then into a different position on the pillows. I know it hurt her. She was good about moving her right shoulder, too." Gwen said, "She and I checked whether the cast was too tight and interfering with her circulation. Fortunately her fingers didn't change color, and she was able to move them easily when I asked her to, several times; when I asked if her fingers felt numb or tingling, she said No." Gwen let out a sigh of relief. "Mrs. Clark will look in on her during the night."

"What's Martha Logan like?" Cherry and Mai Lee asked in the same breath.

"Well, she has a sense of humor, and managed to grin about the pain in her arm and shins," Gwen said. "Her friend, Mrs. Clark, is more upset than she is because—for some urgent professional reason—the trip to England *must* be made on schedule. Fractured arm or not." Gwen looked straight at Cherry. "Dr. Merriam asked me whether I knew of a good nurse who's free for a month to go abroad, and I—well, I—ever helpful..."

"We can guess," Bertha broke in. "You recommended Cherry."

"Well, at least I suggested Cherry as one candidate for the job," Gwen said.

"Thank you for that," Cherry said to Gwen. "But *can* Mrs. Logan go?"

"Dr. Merriam would rather she'd wait and have a good rest," Gwen said, "but she has some very special appointment and says she can't wait. I overheard her say 'No telling when I'd get a second chance *there*.'"

"Where?" said Josie. Gwen shrugged. Cherry sat thinking.

Even if Dr. Merriam decided she was qualified, even if Martha Logan liked her well enough to engage her, would she—in view of the nurse shortage—have the right to go? It was one thing to be on vacation, yet easy to reach in case Hilton Hospital needed her. It was quite another matter to go off to England.

"Will Martha Logan really need a nurse?" Cherry asked Gwen. "If she simply needs a traveling companion, someone to help her dress and take notes and pack, I wouldn't be justified in taking such a job. Not when nurses are so urgently needed on really serious cases."

"Of course she'll need a nurse," Gwen replied. "I guess I didn't make it clear how badly she's hurt.

The dressings on her legs will have to be changed frequently, the arm in the cast observed for any swelling, her general health and diet watched, since she's run down. That's nursing. Actually, Cherry, it's a serious private-duty case, trip or no trip."

Mai Lee said gently, "I appreciate how Cherry feels. The hospital nursing she's been doing is so urgent. On the other hand, Cherry, you need a vacation, so couldn't you look at this assignment as half vacation, half work?"

Gwen said, "I—er—took the liberty of making an appointment for you with Dr. Merriam at his office, tomorrow morning at nine, and with Martha Logan at the Clarks' apartment at ten."

"Wow!" exclaimed Josie. "To think that Cherry might be going to England!"

"How soon?" Cherry said gratefully but weakly. She shook back her dark curls. "It takes time to get a passport and plane reservations and—and—"

"Martha Logan doesn't leave until a week from tomorrow," Gwen said. "You're in luck."

Then Cherry wailed, "Oh, I left my nursing kit home!"

"Lend you mine," said four friendly voices.

"And what will my family say?"

Everyone smiled, knowing Cherry's lively family. If Cherry announced she were going to the moon, her parents and her twin brother Charlie would give her a grand send-off and hide any misgivings. At least this was Gwen's impression of the Ames family, she said.

"Cherry's going to England!" Josie babbled. "Just like that! Oh, my goodness, it's eleven o'clock! Good night!"

They all moved to adjourn. Cherry and Gwen shared one of the small bedrooms, as they used to when all eight—Marie, Ann, Vivian, Mai Lee, Bertha, Josie, Gwen, and Cherry—were visiting nurses in New York. For a long time Cherry lay awake, listening to a neighbor's hi-fi set. She felt excited about the chance to travel abroad, yet half wanted to stay and visit here for a while, then maybe fly up to Quebec for a few days, and then to Washington, D. C., which she loved. She might persuade the Spencer Club to join her for weekends. England seemed far away, and Gwen's recommendation more of a nice try than a real chance to go. Well, tomorrow would decide!

CHAPTER II

Nurse's Vacation

DR. MERRIAM, A SMALL, PREMATURELY GRAY-HAIRED MAN, looked at Cherry with watchful eyes.

"Your nursing record is very good, Miss Ames," he said, when Cherry finished describing her training and experience. "I like the fact that you've tackled so many kinds of nursing jobs and dealt with a variety of people. That should make you a resourceful person for Mrs. Logan to travel with—though I wish she wouldn't travel until she's rested, and recovered from the shock of the fall and fracture. However, she insists on going now, so—if you don't mind, Miss Ames—I'd like to telephone your nursing superintendent at Hilton Hospital for a recommendation."

Cherry said, "Certainly, Doctor," and supplied him with the name and telephone number. He wrote them down.

"On the whole I think you would be a good nurse for this job," he said. "Of course it's up to Mrs. Logan to decide whether you'll be a congenial companion. I'll tell you what. Why don't you nurse her for the next few days? It will give both of you a chance to find out how well you get along. Traveling together could be miserable," Dr. Merriam said with a grin, "if you don't like each other."

Cherry smiled back. "I'd like to try your plan. Is there anything special I need to know about this patient, Doctor?"

"Well, I gather you know she's an author, and Mrs. Clark says a hard-working one. She's a widow with two young children to support—they attend boarding schools. At the moment, I understand, they're with their grandparents until school starts.

"Now, about nursing care," Dr. Merriam continued. "Her hand extending from the cast will have to be watched for swelling. I'll give you a prescription for her, to relieve the pain. See that she rests. Her legs are sore where she bruised them, especially the shins, but there's nothing you can do except change the bandages and wait for the skin to heal. I want her to eat a well-balanced diet. It's necessary after this shock to build up her general health again, if the bone is to heal."

The telephone on the doctor's desk rang. At the same time his white-clad office nurse quietly came in, patients' files in her hand.

"That's all for now, Miss Ames," said Dr. Merriam. "I'll see you at the Clarks' apartment about four this afternoon."

"Thank you, Dr. Merriam," Cherry said, and with a nod at the office nurse, she left.

The Clarks' apartment was only a few blocks away, across Central Park. Cherry walked, enjoying the freshness of the morning and the children playing in the grass and on the swings.

In a big apartment building Cherry took an elevator to the tenth floor and rang the Clarks' doorbell. She was admitted by a maid who doubtfully eyed Cherry's trim red dress, spanking white gloves, and oversize black leather handbag.

"*You* the nurse?"

"Yes, Dr. Merriam sent me. I have my uniform with me," Cherry explained. It was one Gwen had lent her.

A plump woman bustled to the door and said, "Hello, Miss Ames. I'm Alison Clark. We're expecting you," and led Cherry down a hall. Just outside a door that stood open, Mrs. Clark whispered, "Take good care of her. She never takes enough care of herself. It's all I can do to make her stay in bed, even in her condition."

"I'll try my best, Mrs. Clark," Cherry whispered back.

Mrs. Clark led her into a bedroom where a rather tall, slim, short-haired woman lay propped up in bed, a cast on her right forearm. Her clear-cut face was drawn with pain, but even so she had a lively look, and smiled when Mrs. Clark introduced "your new nurse."

"How do you do, Miss Ames?" said Martha Logan. "You are now meeting the most awkward woman of the year, and the world's worst houseguest."

"Martha, do stop being annoyed with yourself," said her friend and hostess. "You aren't used to those steep subway stairs, that's all."

Cherry said very politely, "We could always say someone pushed you."

Mrs. Logan's face lighted up in a grin of pure pleasure. "I see you're a first-rate nurse."

Cherry said, seriously this time, "How do you feel, Mrs. Logan?"

"I hurt," her patient announced. "And I'm astonished at how tired and shaky I feel. Shock, I suppose. I *must* leave for England a week from today, but right now I wonder how I'll ever stand on my poor, battered legs."

"In a week you'll be ever so much better," Cherry said, "providing you cooperate fully with Dr. Merriam and with me," she added assertively.

"I'll cooperate like mad," said Martha Logan. "Miss Ames, can you type? Do you know how to work a tape recorder?"

Mrs. Clark said warningly, "Now, Martha, if this is how you cooperate—"

"But I have to meet a deadline—that book contract I signed day before yesterday—"

Cherry saw how worried Mrs. Logan was about her work, and said, "Yes, I can type, and I know how a tape recorder works. But you'd do better to rest now—really relax all this week. Otherwise, Dr. Merriam may have to tell you not to make your trip. You wouldn't risk going in spite of the doctor's advice, would you?"

Martha Logan's large, grayish-blue eyes turned to two framed photographs on the dresser. One was of a boy of about thirteen, one of a girl aged eleven or twelve. Both children had the same eager, intelligent face as Mrs. Logan, their mother.

She said, "No, I won't do anything foolish."

"Hah!" Mrs. Clark said triumphantly. "Martha, you have met your match in Miss Cherry Ames."

"Where did you get that lovely first name?" Martha Logan asked.

"My parents gave it to me," Cherry said with a straight face, and her patient whooped with laughter. Then Cherry explained she was "sort of named after her grandmother Charity, Cherry for short."

Mrs. Clark said to Martha Logan, "This girl is good for you. I'm relieved to hear you laugh again."

However, so much conversation was tiring the patient, Cherry observed. She caught Mrs. Clark's eye, and they both moved out into the hall, where they discussed meals for Mrs. Logan. Dr. Merriam had ordered a nourishing diet, Mrs. Clark said, but Martha Logan had no appetite.

"We might coax her to eat with smaller portions and more frequent meals," Cherry suggested. "Could she have a cup of hot, rich broth at midmorning, and a glass of milk or ice cream in the afternoon?" Calcium in the milk was needed to help mend the fractured bone. Besides, Cherry thought, Mrs. Logan looked a little spare and underweight.

"We'll do that," Mrs. Clark agreed. "I have a small steak for her at lunch, and broiled chicken for the evening dinner."

"That's fine," Cherry said. She remembered to tell Mrs. Clark that the doctor would come at about four that afternoon. Then Cherry returned to her patient, who was half asleep.

Cherry let her doze while she changed into the crisp white uniform, ventilated the room, opened the borrowed nursing kit, and set up a daily chart for the patient. The doctor would want to see it, and apparently Gwen had not had a chance to do it in yesterday's emergency.

A sleepy voice said, "Oh, I see you've changed into uniform. Hmm, I must really be sick if I have a nurse," Martha Logan said. "You know, in New England where I was born and grew up and went to college, it's considered almost a disgrace to get sick."

Cherry grinned. "In the Middle West where I come from, we have our principles, too, but not as strict as that."

For the first time Cherry saw the woman's basic seriousness. She had already noticed in a corner the books, portable typewriter, tape recorder, notebooks, and box of pencils.

"Well, let's start," Cherry said, "by taking your temperature, pulse, and respiration."

These were about normal, but the pulse was a little slow, and breathing a bit shallow. Cherry recorded the figures on the chart.

The maid brought a cup of beef broth. Cherry held the cup for Mrs. Logan while she reluctantly sipped half of it. Cherry let her rest again, then washed her face and hands, brought her a toothbrush, glass of water and a basin, and after that, combed her hair. Mrs. Clark had tried to tidy her up earlier that morning but, Martha Logan admitted, was not too expert at it. "I feel much fresher now," she said. "Almost human again." Cherry did not suggest a bed bath nor even changing into a fresh nightgown, since her patient felt quite weak. Cherry did ask her to move her arm into a different position on the pillows, and to move her fingers.

Cherry let her rest again before gently removing the dressings on her bruised, scraped legs and left arm, and applying clean gauze dressings. Mrs. Logan bit her lip, but all she said was, "The only ache I *haven't* got is a toothache." By this time Mrs. Clark came in to ask if she might serve lunch. Cherry coaxed her patient to eat a few bites of steak and vegetables, but Martha Logan murmured, "I only want to sleep." Cherry let her alone, and slipped into another room to have the sandwich that Mrs. Clark thoughtfully provided for her.

"How do you think she is, Miss Cherry?"

"Weaker and more shaken up than she realizes, I'm afraid, Mrs. Clark."

"Yes, Martha never 'pampers' herself, as she calls it. She has tremendous spirit," her friend said.

Cherry had a glimpse of that spirit later that afternoon when Martha Logan talked about her children. She had awakened refreshed, and Cherry, after checking her TPR, was giving her a back rub.

"Ruthie is almost twelve," Mrs. Logan said, "good at sports and all her school activities. I suspect she finds my books dry, although she loyally reads each one as it comes out. So does her brother. Bob is thirteen, and he has a scientific turn of mind, a real talent as his father did—"

She hesitated, and Cherry filled in the pause. "From their photographs, they look like fine children."

"They're good, self-reliant people, young as they are. They were just babies when their father died."

In a direct but reserved way Mrs. Logan said Kenneth Logan had died suddenly after a short illness. He had been a research scientist for one of the big utilities companies. Cherry thought they could not have been married very long, for Martha Logan was still a youthful woman. She was attractive, too—not exactly pretty, but very feminine and pleasant. Mrs. Logan abruptly changed the subject.

"Do you read much, Cherry?"

"As much as I have time for, Mrs. Logan, after keeping abreast of new medical discoveries. I love to read. I'm embarrassed to admit I haven't yet read your books, but I shall. My friend Mai Lee is reading your latest book."

"You're an honest girl," Martha Logan remarked. "Ouch! My arm! My aching, poor old writing arm!"

"I'll give you a delicious tablet," said Cherry, uncapping the bottle. "Try to rest. No more talking, now. No, ma'am, no reading, not just yet. You'll feel better if you rest." She darkened the room.

At four o'clock Dr. Merriam arrived, somewhat out of breath. He checked over his patient and conferred briefly with Cherry. He was satisfied with Mrs. Logan's progress, and had no new instructions for the nurse. But Martha had an announcement for both of them.

"When I fly to England next week, Dr. Merriam, I'd like to take this young nurse with me. I realize I'm in no condition to travel alone, and I understood from you she's on vacation for a month, anyway."

"Now just a minute!" Dr. Merriam said. "First it's a question of whether you'll be able to go—"

"I have an appointment to see the Carewe collection, which is harder to get, I hear, than being received at court," Martha Logan said rather desperately. "It took me months and much effort to get a letter of admission. If I don't keep the appointment, I may never get into the museum at all! For my next book I *must* see that collection!"

The doctor threw up his hands. Mrs. Logan turned her head on the pillows to look at Cherry. "I know this is sudden, but I generally come to a quick decision. Would you like to go? Frankly, I can't afford to pay for both your travel expenses *and* a salary for your nursing services on the trip. The most I can pay for is your transportation, hotel, and meals—and that's only because my publisher has been kind enough to advance me some extra funds. We'll keep our travel expenses on a modest budget. No glittering luxuries, but it will be very nice. And very interesting."

Cherry took a deep breath. "Wouldn't you rather wait a few days to think this over, Mrs. Logan?"

"No, I'm sure now about you," Martha Logan said. "But I want *you* to take a day or two to think it over."

Cherry grinned. "I'm sure, too. I'd be perfectly delighted to go!"

Dr. Merriam started to laugh. "I see that you two understand each other! And I see there's no holding you back, Mrs. Logan. I reluctantly give permission. Well, Miss Ames, you'd better get busy arranging for your trip. A week—six days, rather—isn't much time to prepare to go abroad."

Martha Logan said she would ask the Clarks to telephone her travel agent to make reservations for Cherry. It would not be easy, at such short notice, to get a seat for Cherry on the same plane, especially an adjoining seat. Cancellations did occur, though, and a travel agent often could make better arrangements than a private individual.

"Have you a passport?" Martha Logan asked Cherry, who shook her head. "You'd better hurry and get one. You'll need your birth certificate."

"I have a photostat of it with me," Cherry said, "because I thought I might be going to Quebec." Americans are not required to have a passport to enter Canada, but must show some proof of American citizenship in order to re-enter the United States.

"You'll need vaccination against smallpox, and an international certificate of vaccination," Dr. Merriam said to Cherry. "Call my office for an appointment. Now I must go, Mrs. Logan. Try to relax, and I'll come in again soon."

After the doctor left, Cherry and Mrs. Logan looked at each other in satisfaction. They laughed out of sheer exuberance.

"We'll have a wonderful trip!" Martha Logan said. "Young lady, for the next few days you'd better nurse me with one hand—and apply yourself to getting ready for takeoff with the other."

"Everything will get done," Cherry said calmly, hiding her excitement, "and I'll nurse you with both hands."

However, for the next few days Cherry had to move at top speed. She telephoned her family long distance that evening to tell them her news, and see what they thought of it. "Why, of course, go!" her father said, and her mother said, "Honey, I'm so happy for you!" Charlie was working in Indianapolis. Cherry tried to telephone him there. Unfortunately he was away on business, but she knew her twin would be all for her trip. Her Spencer Club friends certainly were for it. They practically danced in excitement and glee for her, and they offered to lend her uniforms, nursing kits, clothes, cameras, anything they had.

"Thanks ever so much," Cherry said, "but Mother will mail me my nursing things and some clothes—via special handling, so they'll come fast."

Early Friday morning Cherry went to the Passport Office in Rockefeller Center. A clerk gave her the necessary application to fill out, and instructions, and promised to rush her passport through. Then Cherry went downstairs and sat while passport photographs were taken, to be called for after they were developed. She hurried uptown and took care of Mrs. Logan, who seemed a little better today.

Mrs. Clark reported that the travel agent was attempting to make a flight reservation for Cherry, and thought they had a good chance. The forthcoming weekend was Labor Day weekend, and after that big holiday, the summer travel rush abated.

Cherry was giving Mrs. Logan morning care when her patient suddenly remembered something.

"We've got to send a cable to the Carewe Museum about you, Cherry," Martha said. "Otherwise, they may not let you come in with me. Can you give me the names and addresses of two or three persons, preferably of some official or professional standing, who can swear that you're a solid citizen?"

Cherry could, but she had never heard of a private museum so fussy that visitors had to furnish character references. Martha Logan explained, "This is Mr. Carewe's private mansion, his collection is priceless, and anyway, I hear he's rather peculiar—"

Cherry was intrigued. She sent the cable while her patient had an afternoon nap. Then two friends, Mr. and Mrs. Le Sueuer, came to visit Mrs. Logan. They were curious about the Carewe Museum—as curious as Cherry herself.

"I've heard it's a fabulous place," Mrs. Le Sueuer said. "But why? And why is it so hard to be admitted?"

So Martha Logan explained. This celebrated collection of paintings included famous personages of several centuries, portrayed by great artists. The collection was priceless—any art museum, certainly any art dealer or private collector, would be overjoyed to own one or two of its treasures. John Carewe had inherited some of the paintings, long in his mother's family. Being many times a millionaire and a shrewd businessman, he had augmented the collection by acquisitions—by purchases or "horse trading"—during his long lifetime.

Newspapers regularly complained that Carewe selfishly kept for his private enjoyment a collection that should be open to public view. John Carewe retorted he felt no obligation to the public. The collection remained closed, locked up for weeks and months on end. Very rarely was the Carewe Museum open to visitors, and then only by screening applicants who sent a letter of request for admission. Very few applicants got in.

"I've heard Carewe is an eccentric," Martha Logan said to the Le Sueuers and Cherry. Mr. Le Sueuer shook his head in amazement.

The Carewe collection was housed, Martha said, in a mansion on a country estate. It was guarded by a high wall, an electric burglar-alarm system, and a staff of caretakers and guards.

"An impossible place to enter without a letter of admission," Martha Logan said, "because Mr. Carewe insists applicants furnish references, which he and his staff thoroughly check. It takes an awfully long time for an applicant to get an answer, because Mr. Carewe often is abroad, and he will not entrust a final decision to any secretary or staff member or even his museum curator. I applied months ago. And now"—Martha Logan smiled at Cherry—"I just hope they'll admit my nurse with me."

Cherry hoped so, too. She also hoped the visitors would leave soon, before they tired her patient. Fortunately the Le Sueuers had another appointment, and stayed only until their friend opened the *bon voyage* present they had brought her. "Just what any writer would want—a good book," Martha Logan said, thanking them.

Cherry left nursing duty early, with Mrs. Clark taking over, and hurried downtown to Rockefeller Center. She picked up her perfectly awful passport photos ("Even my own mother wouldn't recognize it's me," Cherry thought, wincing), and brought photos, filled-out application blanks, and fee upstairs to the Passport Office. She gave these to the same clerk, and showed him the photostat of her birth certificate. Everything was in order now. He told her to call for her passport early the next week, since time was too short to mail it.

On her way home, Cherry stopped in at Dr. Merriam's office to be vaccinated. He said:

"This is as good a time as any to give you a few instructions, Miss Ames, for the trip. While you are in London, take Mrs. Logan to consult Dr. Bates— Dr. Alan Bates." He wrote down an address and gave it to Cherry. "Try to make the appointment within two weeks from the date of her accident. Dr. Bates will X-ray the arm to see whether it is healing properly. Ask him to look at those scraped shins, too."

"Yes, Dr. Merriam," said Cherry.

"By four weeks after her accident, X-rays will be required again, and it probably will be time to remove the cast. At that time," Dr. Merriam added, "Mrs. Clark tells me, you will be in Edinburgh—"

Cherry's heart gave a leap. She hadn't known they were going on to Scotland.

"—where there are wonderful medical talents and facilities. Ask Dr. Bates to refer you to a doctor in Edinburgh." Cherry nodded. "Once the cast is off, Miss Ames, you'll need to assist Mrs. Logan in exercising the arm daily. You may also need to massage the arm and shoulder as well. That will depend on what the Edinburgh doctor decides."

"I understand, Dr. Merriam. I've been working on the Orthopedics Ward at Hilton Hospital."

"Good. Oh, one more thing. Take along a few simple remedies—something for an upset stomach, or headache, just in case." He wrote out a prescription. "See that Mrs. Logan has frequent rest periods, she must not walk or stand too long at a time. That should do it for now, Miss Ames."

On Saturday, after the usual morning care, Cherry encouraged Mrs. Logan to move her right arm and shoulder at regular intervals. After a rest, she helped her patient get used to using her left arm and hand,

starting with combing her hair. The result was ludi-
crous. "It's your first try," Cherry said. "But you'll see,
practice makes perfect."

She coaxed Martha Logan to eat lunch and settled
her for a nap. Later in the afternoon she gave her a bed
bath, and after that, at Mrs. Logan's request, put some
business papers in order. Since Martha Logan was
right-handed and had broken her right arm, Cherry
was going to have to do paperwork and take notes for
her during the trip.

Late that afternoon the travel agent telephoned.
He had gotten a cancellation for Cherry. Now the airline people were trying to get some other passenger to
trade seats, so Mrs. Logan could have her nurse beside
her. "Cheers!" said Martha Logan.

Just before Cherry was to go off duty, Dr. Merriam
hurried in. The doctor and the nurse helped Mrs.
Logan to get to her feet. Cherry was surprised to see
that she was taller than she had appeared to be in bed.
At first she was weak and unsteady. She sat up in a
chair for a while, and walked better on the second try.
The doctor and Cherry discussed the importance of
not allowing their patient to grow stiff and weak from
lying in bed. "Help her to walk over the weekend," Dr.
Merriam reminded Cherry, although she needed no
reminding.

Cherry and her patient practiced, and they also grew
better acquainted during the quiet of Sunday and Labor
Day, Cherry's mother had sent her a special-delivery
letter, and Cherry read the more interesting parts of it

aloud to her patient. Mrs. Logan wanted to hear more, so Cherry told her a little about her parents in Hilton, where she was born and grew up, and about her twin brother who was an aviation engineer. "They must be a good family," Mrs. Logan said, "to have produced you. You know, I'd like to call you Cherry. And I'd like you to call me Martha. I know it's against protocol for nurses to address patients by their first names, but since we'll be traveling companions for a month, it will seem so much friendlier. Now please tell me more about your wonderful family."

But Cherry was careful not to talk too much or too constantly. Martha Logan still felt badly shaken up and on this hot day the cast felt uncomfortably tight. Cherry gave her medication and left her alone to rest.

Later, she took out the rubber ball she had brought with her. She gave it to Mrs. Logan, explaining, "It would be a good idea for you to squeeze this ball for about ten or fifteen minutes at a time, four or five times a day. It will help your arm muscles to keep their tone. We'll work into it gradually. Want to try? I'll help you, until you can manage by yourself."

They worked with the ball and Cherry also encouraged Martha to move her shoulders, and praised her. At one interval, Martha told Cherry: "We'll go to the airport a little early on Thursday morning. A reporter has made an appointment with me. He's bringing a photographer who wants a picture of us boarding the plane."

"Good promotion for your next book," said Cherry.

"My publisher thinks so," Martha replied. "There already was one news item in the papers when I arrived in New York, saying I'm on my way to England to do research and visit the celebrated Carewe collection for the next book. I expect the reporter saw that news story, because he called up my publisher to find out where I'm staying in New York. The publisher referred him to me. I said okay to the interview, and told him my flight date, hour, and number."

"What newspaper is he with?" Cherry asked.

"This man—Blake or Blakeley, I forget which—is a freelance reporter who writes occasional special-interest stories for the *London Evening Times* and other newspapers here and abroad. Such reporters are called stringers, aren't they? Anyway," Martha said, "they supply local items to out-of-town newspapers, and they hire their own photographers."

Cherry asked what masterpieces in the Carewe collection she particularly wanted to see.

"Well, this is to be a historical novel," said Martha, "about—" and she named an English nobleman and two ladies, sisters, who had figured in his long eventful service to his embattled country. "In the Carewe collection there are portraits of all three of them. Even better, there are *two* portraits of Henry—one when he was young, and one when much older. I want to see how he changed, in character. I want to study the faces in the portraits for more understanding of those persons. I want to see how they stand and sit—whether their bearing is humble or proud or defiant, or what. And

I want to study the details of their dress, because dress reveals character, too. I'm especially interested in a ring of Lady Mary's that disappeared mysteriously—perhaps given as ransom. I've heard she wears it in the Carewe-owned portrait."

Martha was a scholarly person, without being tiresome about it. The past sprang to life as she talked of ancient places and long-dead personages as if they were old friends of hers. During the holiday weekend Cherry learned a great deal and enjoyed it.

Tuesday brought people bustling back to work, on regular busy schedules, and it brought Cherry requests from Martha Logan to shop and pack for her. Doing this, in addition to nursing, picking up her passport, consulting with Dr. Merriam one final time, buying travelers' checks, changing a few dollars into English currency for immediate taxi fares and tips, then going to the hairdresser and doing her own packing, kept Cherry racing until late Wednesday evening. She had to be at the Clarks' apartment early the next morning in order to help Martha Logan dress and check her over once more.

That night Cherry said her goodbyes to her Spencer Club friends and telephoned her mother and father to ask, "What presents shall I bring you?" She laid out her nurse's uniform, cap, and nursing kit for the next morning. When at last she tumbled into bed, she felt too excited to sleep. This time tomorrow she would be in London!

CHAPTER III

Flight to London

THE SUN SHONE DOWN ON THE AIRPORT AND ON THE jetliner waiting just outside the terminal. It was nine fifteen, forty-five minutes before takeoff. Mrs. Clark, who had driven Cherry and her patient to Idlewild, pulled in at the second-floor level of the terminal. A porter took their baggage, and waited.

Cherry in her white uniform and an airlines steward helped Mrs. Logan out of the car and into a wheelchair. Cherry had telephoned ahead for the wheelchair. Martha Logan was still stiff from her fall, and Dr. Merriam advised against her walking across the big terminal and then the walkway into the plane.

"Alison," Martha Logan said to her friend, "it will be a nuisance for you to park the car and walk back across that huge parking lot, to return to the terminal just to see me off. Let's say our goodbyes now, my dear. Thank you for everything."

"Bon voyage," said Mrs. Clark, and leaned out of the car to kiss her. "Enjoy yourselves, both of you. I know Cherry will take good care of you." Mrs. Clark waved and drove off.

Cherry and the porter followed the steward pushing Martha in the wheelchair. In the terminal he helped them quickly check their baggage through. Cherry tipped the porter, and they moved to the next counter where they showed their tickets. Then, at Mrs. Logan's request, the steward wheeled her to just below the centrally located Flight Information Board. Cherry, carrying a small canvas flight bag, looked up and read: FLIGHT 160 10:00 A.M. GATE 6. "That's *us!*" she thought.

"Thank you very much," Cherry said to the young steward. "The photographer should get a fine picture of Mrs. Logan here."

"Not in the wheelchair!" Martha groaned. "Although it is a great comfort," she said to the steward. He asked if there were anything further he could do for them and promised to return to help them board.

They waited for the reporter and his photographer. Cherry thought Martha Logan looked most attractive in her soft-colored, lightweight tweeds, and what's more, looked well. Cherry said so. Martha smiled and thanked her for the compliment.

"You look positively radiant with health," Martha said. "And that fetching cap and trim uniform! I wish Ruth and Bobby could meet you."

Cherry said she hoped to meet the Logan children some time. "Speaking of time—" Martha glanced at her wristwatch and said, "That reporter is late."

More minutes went by, the food trucks finished loading the plane, and the passengers were entering at the open glass door marked Gate 6. Still no reporter or photographer. Cherry asked if Mrs. Logan wanted her to go look for them, or telephone the reporter.

"I don't know where to telephone him, since he's not on the staff of any newspaper," Mrs. Logan said. "As for looking for him, there's no point. I clearly said nine thirty and at this spot. Well, I guess he's not coming," she said matter-of-factly. "Maybe something unexpectedly detained him."

The same young steward returned to ask if Mrs. Logan was ready to board now. He would push her wheelchair along the walkway that led directly to the plane's cabin. He suggested they start before all the other hundred or so passengers poured in.

"A good idea," Martha Logan said. "I don't enjoy being interviewed, anyway."

They started along the walkway, Cherry going first, then the steward carefully pushing her patient. Halfway across, the wheelchair balked for some reason. A short, portly man ahead of Cherry turned around. Before she could do it, he bent and adjusted one wheel with his left hand,

"A little slower there, steward!" he ordered. Cherry felt embarrassed for the obliging young steward. Standing up again, the man looked imposing. "Are you all right, madam?"

"Yes, thank you," Martha Logan said.

As they entered the plane cabin's door, the short, portly man gave a little assistance again, even before the stewardess could. Then with a slight bow he left them and went to his seat.

The stewardess greeted them and helped Cherry get Martha Logan to her feet. "I feel so conspicuous," Martha grumbled to Cherry, "and clumsy as an ox."

"You're not, and anyway, must you expect miracles of yourself?" Cherry murmured back. Better to jolly her patient than offer too much sympathy.

Martha Logan grinned and refused to take Cherry's arm. After thanking the steward again, she walked slowly down the plane aisle. Cherry followed close behind her and found their numbered seats. Fortunately, Martha had an aisle seat. Cherry got her comfortably settled. Because of the cast, Cherry had a little difficulty in fastening the seat belt around her patient's waist. Another stewardess came and helped, took their coats, and said the cabin crew was at their service.

Cherry, seated at Martha Logan's left, watched the plane fill up. Music played and the passengers, mostly Americans, a few English and Canadians, seemed festive. On Cherry's left, an elderly man dozed beside the plane window. Across the aisle a brisk young American took business reports out of his briefcase; beyond him sat a reserved-looking middle-aged couple. Cherry thought their nearest seatmates probably would not want much conversation, and that was just as well for her patient.

Or was it? Martha Logan was watching everyone with alert, sparkling eyes. "Grand to be out in the world again," she said to Cherry, "after being confined to a sickroom." Martha pointed out the man who had helped them on the walkway. He sat four seats ahead, on the opposite aisle. "He's keeping the stewardesses busy with his requests," she remarked.

An extremely pleasant-looking young man came in and stowed a string bag, filled with books, under the seat ahead of Martha Logan. He glanced at her inquisitively, then at Cherry in her nurse's uniform. Cherry didn't know him, but thought he might turn out to be a lively traveling companion. He was nice-looking in an unexceptional way—he was of medium height, brown-haired, and he wore glasses—and he had a friendly, breezy energetic air about him that Cherry liked.

"Excuse me, is this yours?" he said, and handed Martha her scarf, which had fallen under his seat. He gave Cherry an admiring look and reluctantly sat down. Martha seemed amused; she noticed everything.

Promptly at ten o'clock the jetliner took off, rising like a giant bird. After several minutes' climbing into the brilliant blue sky, the plane leveled off. It flew out over the Atlantic, east toward the sun. Cherry unfastened her seat belt, and Mrs. Logan's, and took her patient's pulse. It was normal.

"How do you feel?" Cherry asked. Cherry knew that Martha must walk up and down the plane aisle at least once every hour, to avoid stiffness.

"I feel wonderful," Martha said.... "Well, yes, my arm aches."

Cherry reached for a pillow from the rack overhead, to prop under the aching arm. Instantly the breezy-looking young man in the seat ahead jumped up as Cherry stood up. "Let me help you," he said. "I—uh—I'm the one who swapped seats with you at the airline's request so you could sit together—so I'm sort of interested." Cherry smiled at him and sat down.

At eleven, after Martha had rested, Cherry took her for the first slow, uncertain walk along the plane aisle. The plane rolled only very slightly. Her shaky patient managed to walk. A few passengers glanced up, and the young steward hurried to assist, but Cherry shook her head. As the injured woman and her nurse neared his seat, the important-looking little man rose and offered Martha Logan "a moment's rest in my seat." She smiled and declined.

An hour later, at noon, when they attempted the walk again, the man rose and deferentially spoke to them.

"I beg your pardon, madam, but I've long been a great admirer of your books. Aren't you Martha Logan? I believe I recognize you from the photograph on the book jackets."

Martha colored with pleasure. "How very kind of you."

"Would it be an imposition if—it would mean so much to me to chat with you for a few minutes—unless," the man glanced tactfully at Cherry, "your nurse feels it would tire you?"

"Not at all," Martha answered. "I'd be delighted to have some conversation."

After they resumed their seats, the portly little man came and stood in the aisle beside them. He presented Mrs. Logan with his card—his name was Archibald Hazard. Martha introduced him to Cherry, and he gave her a charming, if faintly condescending, smile.

He was a New Yorker, an economist, on the staff of a magazine in that field, he said briefly. "But my private enthusiasm is art and art history. Particularly those of England. You can imagine, Mrs. Logan, how much enjoyment your distinguished books give me."

Mr. Hazard seemed rather distinguished himself, Cherry thought, as the other two conversed. Mr. Hazard also seemed to possess an impressive knowledge of art, judging from Martha's interest in what he said. Yes, he had often been abroad; yes, sometimes collecting a few works of art, he admitted, "but chiefly for study and the refreshment of travel and to see my friends.

"Tell me, Mrs. Logan," he asked, "what do you think of the historical portraits in the Queen's Gallery at Buckingham Palace?"

Martha Logan said she admired the Rembrandt and Holbein portraits very much, then asked his opinion about other paintings in the collection. Cherry noticed that Mr. Hazard quickly, deftly changed the subject.

Martha did not seem to mind, but Cherry wondered. Was he pretending to know more than he actually did?

They were deep in conversation, agreeing, disagreeing, comparing notes. In the seat ahead the young man's head was cocked out in the aisle as if he were listening—until a stewardess came by carrying lunch trays. The stewardess wanted to serve the injured passenger first. Mr. Hazard seemed to be annoyed at the interruption, thanked Martha Logan, and excused himself.

"He's an interesting man," Martha said, as Cherry cut up her meat for her. "It's fun finding an art enthusiast on the plane!"

"Well, cheers," Cherry said, "and now please try to eat something." Her patient, still remarking on the conversation, had to be coaxed, all but fed. After lunch Cherry opened the small canvas flight bag she had packed with a few comforts for her patient, took out soft knitted slippers, and helped Martha put them on.

"How you spoil me," her patient said. "I feel like an overgrown infant. Don't be surprised if I give forth with baby talk."

"You'll be self-reliant soon," Cherry said. "Try to sleep now," she advised, offering her dark glasses. The light up here above the clouds was brilliant, though less bright than before. In fact, although Cherry's wristwatch—on New York time, Eastern Daylight Saving Time—read one o'clock, actually noon, outside it looked like midafternoon.

Her patient napped for only about twenty minutes. Then Cherry slipped Martha's shoes on for her, and they started for a shaky walk again. This time, the young man in the seat ahead gave Martha a hand as the plane swayed. In his quick movement, he dropped his book, and Martha noticed it was a mystery story.

"I love these," she said to the young man. Cherry looked surprised. "Oh, yes, I put two mysteries into my big suitcase when you weren't looking. You know, tracking down historical facts that are half lost is a kind of detective work."

"I've read your historical novels, Mrs. Logan," the young man said. "In fact, I assign them to my classes for background reading. I'm Peter Holt. I teach English literature at—" He named a state university in the Northwest.

"What—not American literature?" Cherry asked teasingly.

"That's a point," Martha Logan said, laughing. "This is Cherry Ames, Mr. Holt. She bullies me into walking. Come and talk to us after our parade."

They moved off. Most of the passengers were dozing after lunch. Cherry noticed that Mr. Hazard was asleep. A stewardess came and asked if Mrs. Logan or her nurse needed anything, but Cherry answered, "No, thanks." On their return to their seats, Martha seemed ready to rest. Cherry settled her comfortably, and in a few minutes she closed her eyes.

Someone whispered, "Can you come out and talk to me?" It was Peter Holt. Cherry decided her patient might sleep for a while, so she crawled past her and followed the young man. They went to stand in an open area at the end of the cabin. She could watch Martha from there.

"I was surprised to hear you're a professor," Cherry said. "Aren't professors supposed to be old and solemn?"

"I'll be old eventually," he assured her. "In the meantime, I'm only an assistant professor."

"Are you terribly learned?"

"Well, I have a Ph.D., but I ask my students not to call me 'doctor.' Plain 'mister' is good enough. I'm on my way to meet a dozen of my students now," he volunteered. "We're taking a student tour through England. They went ahead on a charter plane, with the Kimball kids' parents as chaperones temporarily—I was delayed, I had to take care of some business for my mother. I'll meet the students in London and take over."

"A student tour sounds like a wonderful way to study," Cherry said. "Where are you going?"

Peter described their three-week itinerary—a stay in London, on to Shakespeare's Stratford-upon-Avon, north through the Lake Country of Wordsworth, and finally into Scotland to Edinburgh.

"We'll go on bicycles part of the way. I've done that before," he said, his face bright with the memory. "We'll fly home just in time for the opening of the fall semester."

"Your itinerary is much the same as Mrs. Logan's and mine," Cherry said.

"I hope we'll see each other along the way."

They compared the timing of their routes. It seemed possible they would meet. "At least perhaps in London, these next few days," Peter Holt said. Cherry told him the name of their hotel, sure her employer would not mind. He said, "You know, I'd like a chance to get to know Martha Logan a little. Her work is—"

"Oh-ho, so it's not me you'd like to see again," Cherry teased.

Peter simply grinned and shook his head. "Mrs. Logan is charming, but she's not my reason." He looked squarely at Cherry. "By the way, have you noticed the honeymoon couple sitting next to me? Their clothes are brand new; she's wearing orchids or something; and they're so absorbed in each other they don't know the other passengers exist. Ah, well, I'm for romance."

Cherry smiled and said nothing. Their conversation hung there, unfinished. She peered down the aisle. "Excuse me, but I think Mrs. Logan is awake now."

They started to their seats. Martha looked refreshed, and remarked on how rapidly the afternoon was fading. The clouds below them glowed with sunset reflections as the plane flew ahead into a dusk-darkened sky. It was two o'clock by Cherry's wristwatch. Martha had already set her watch five hours forward to London time.

They took another slow, unsteady walk. Mr. Hazard rose to ask if he might come back to continue their chat. On returning to their seats, they found Mr. Hazard persuading the brisk young businessman across the aisle to trade seats with him for a while.

This time Peter Holt joined in the conversation, perched on the arm of his seat. Martha introduced the young man to Archibald Hazard, who half ignored him. Perhaps Mr. Hazard felt entitled to a monopoly on Martha Logan's attention, Cherry thought, and did not want Peter's competition. For Peter more than held his own in their far-ranging conversation. Peter outshone the older man, who cut him short by saying:

"Do you plan to be in London long, Mrs. Logan?"

"For about a week," she replied.

"So shall I. Then possibly to Paris. You, too?"

"No, a leisurely trip through central England—Oxford, Stratford-upon-Avon, the Midlands, up to Lake Windermere to the Carewe Museum—"

"The Carewe Museum!" Mr. Hazard interrupted her. "What a privilege! How I envy your having entree there! Such a jealously guarded collection. I've never even *tried* to get in."

"Well, I suppose they'd never have let me in, either," Martha said, "except that I need to see those famous old portraits for my next book."

"I've heard," Mr. Hazard said, "that John Carewe is an eccentric and one must write far in advance for a card of admission, and then, there's a tremendous, long-winded fuss about references. Did that character give you a specific date for your visit?"

"Oh, very specific." At this, Mr. Hazard raised his eyebrows. He looked so amused and interested that Martha Logan said, "We are to visit on Monday, September twenty-third, at exactly ten o'clock in the morning, and we are allowed to stay no more than two hours. Oh, yes, I was required to give references. I still don't know whether they'll let my nurse come in with me."

Archibald Hazard laughed so hard that his potbelly shook.

"Yes, I've heard other stories like that about the legendary John Carewe," Peter said. He and Cherry had been left out of the conversation. Martha turned to include them.

"Have you, Mr. Holt? Well, possibly Mr. Carewe *is* eccentric," Martha Logan said, "or perhaps he's just taking no chances of being robbed."

"I believe he was robbed once, about ten years ago," Archibald Hazard put in. "Fortunately, the thieves were caught very quickly, and the paintings recovered. Undamaged."

"Oh, really?" Martha said. "That might explain his being so careful about whom he admits. I hear Mr. Carewe will not honor every application. He's very selective, or choosy, or whatever else you want to call it."

"He's frankly a snob," Mr. Hazard declared. "He wants only distinguished visitors. I heard an art dealer quote Carewe as saying he 'won't waste his time on commonplace visitors who fail to appreciate works of art.' You, Miss Cherry, had better wear ermine and emeralds instead of your nurse's uniform, or the old man may not admit you."

Cherry and Peter began to laugh. The conversation was interrupted by the stewardesses serving light refreshments. Peter had to take his seat. It was evening now, and in London it was half past eight. But it was half past three by Cherry's wristwatch and by her stomach. She and Martha declined the refreshments, and when the aisle was clear, went for their hourly walk.

"Our walk is late," Martha said, "we talked so much. Mr. Hazard certainly is interesting company."

"I suppose so," Cherry said, "but don't let him tire you. I wish he wouldn't lead you to talk so much."

"His interest is perfectly natural in an art lover," Martha defended him. "I'm enjoying talking with him."

Resuming their places, they found Mr. Hazard had stayed in his borrowed seat, across the aisle. His tray was barely touched.

"Vile food," he complained, "invariably awful on every airline." Martha remarked that she thought the food quite good, and what better did he expect six miles up? "I suppose I am spoiled," he conceded. "Our family always had a first-rate chef in the kitchen, so I am a stickler about food."

They talked about the fine restaurants in London, and then about London's art collections. Peter Holt tried to join the conversation, but Mr. Hazard snubbed him and managed to monopolize both ladies. In embarrassment Cherry smiled at the young man, and Martha made a point of giving Peter her undivided attention. Cherry turned to Mr. Hazard and asked him about something interesting she'd read of late in the newspapers—a controversy going on among art historians, as to whether certain Michelangelo drawings were not actually done by other artists. Mr. Hazard just looked blank. Then he remarked that such discussions bored him, and glanced away.

"Hmm," Cherry thought. "This is the second time Mr. Hazard has avoided answering a direct question. He doesn't know nearly as much as he'd like us to believe. The old faker, posing as an art connoisseur!"

She wondered whether Martha Logan had noticed, but she was absorbed in talking with Peter. Mr. Hazard made a fresh bid for her attention, by naming modern painters whose work was currently being displayed for sale by London art dealers.

Mrs. Logan was immediately interested. "You do keep up with the art news, don't you, Mr. Hazard?"

"I'm acquainted with several art dealers in New York," Archibald Hazard said, "and, well, in many parts of the world. And I subscribe to the London newspapers to keep informed about art news there."

"I happen to know an art dealer in London," Martha Logan responded. "Pierre Selsam, who owns the Selsam Gallery in Mayfair."

"Oh, really? Possibly you know," Mr. Hazard said, "that he's showing a million dollars' worth of French Impressionists—ten Renoirs, several Cézannes, as well as Picassos and other important works. Be sure to see Selsam's exhibit."

"I shall, thanks. In fact, I hope to see Pierre Selsam during the week we'll be in London," Martha Logan replied.

"And don't miss the show of young painters at the Bonney Gallery, the best young hopefuls in many seasons, according to the critics and the way private collectors are buying—"

Cherry grew restless. Around her, the other passengers were collecting their belongings and filling out the landing cards that the stewardesses had distributed. Cherry filled out her patient's and her own cards. She whispered to Mrs. Logan:

"Would you like me to walk you to the washroom, to freshen up for our arrival?"

"Yes, Cherry. Please excuse us, Mr. Hazard."

As they came back, the plane was gradually losing altitude. Ahead and below in the dark lay a few tiny, scattered lights—the coast of England. The pilot announced over the P.A. system, "Ladies and gentlemen, we will be landing at London Airport in twenty minutes." The young steward advised Cherry that a wheelchair would be brought for her patient. Peter Holt, clutching his books, turned around to say:

"I'd like to be of service to you ladies, if I may— starting right now."

Martha thanked him, but Mr. Hazard insisted in his lordly way that *he* be allowed to see them off the plane, through Customs, and safely into a taxi. Peter looked disappointed.

By the time they went through Immigration Service, Peter Holt was being carried off by his students, anyway, Cherry noticed. Mr. Hazard, who was being a great help, found them a taxi, saw to their luggage, and helped them in. He said he was staying at the other side of London from them, at the Ritz, but he escorted them to their hotel. When Martha tried to thank him for being so attentive, he would not hear of it.

"Call me at the Ritz if I can be of further service," he said. "I hope you and Miss Ames will have lunch with me soon."

"I'll look forward to it," Martha said warmly, and Cherry smiled her best. She'd rather have lunch or just a walk with Peter Holt—but maybe that would happen, too.

CHAPTER IV

An Eventful Week

"MAKE HASTE SLOWLY," CHERRY CAUTIONED HER PATIENT on their first day in London. Martha Logan, eager to see her British publisher and friends, was exasperated that she must move slowly. The most Cherry thought it wise for her to do was to make telephone calls. Cherry also telephoned for an appointment for her to see the doctor later in their stay. Cherry unpacked for her and unpacked her own clothes. She would wear street clothes, not her white uniform, during the trip. She put on a white apron, scrubbed her hands, and changed the dressings on her patient's legs.

Then they ventured out on London's stately, historic streets to go to a restaurant for lunch, but the crowds tired Martha. On their return Cherry insisted they remain quietly in their adjoining rooms for the rest of the day.

Martha Logan was restless until an unexpectedly entertaining program turned up on the television set that she had rented to use in her room. She and Cherry watched a half-hour interview with Shah Liddy, a flamboyant, white-bearded plump little man who had just arrived in England with his wife for a visit of three or possibly four weeks. The title "Shah" was honorary. Basil Liddy was an Englishman who had lived most of his life in the Near East and had amassed a great fortune there. He was famous as an avid art patron and collector. He sported—besides his luxuriant white beard, a mustache, and bristling white eyebrows—a flower in his buttonhole, a pipe, and he spoke with an Oxford accent. A *bon vivant,* he talked enthusiastically of fine foods and wines, as well as of paintings. Lady Liddy was a pretty blond young Englishwoman, much younger than the Shah, who quietly let her theatrical husband do most of the talking.

"Isn't he a character!" Martha exclaimed, when the telecast was over. "His collection sounds fabulous— but that beard! Speaking of interviews, I wonder why that reporter never showed up at Idlewild to interview me. Probably because I don't wear a white beard."

On Saturday they were still careful not to overdo, but did go outdoors for a short time on this fine day. Cherry had deep, special feelings about London. Here in this ancient city, founded by the Romans, were so many of the things she had read and heard about—London Bridge of the nursery rhyme, the Magna Carta, the first document to declare the principles for democratic government and a free citizenry, and along the River Thames the place where Shakespeare had rehearsed his Globe Theater players. Here stood Westminster Abbey where centuries of England's kings and poets reposed in stone vaults; here was Keats's nightingale still singing in her memory up on Hampstead Heath hill, and here were the houses on crowded lanes where Dickens's characters lived. Martha Logan said she felt the same way, no matter how often she came to London.

Yet this was a thoroughly modern, fast-paced city, not startlingly different from American cities, except for the double-decker red buses. Cherry found British accents and currency a little foreign to her, as they shopped for presents to send home. Cherry chose Liberty silk scarfs for her mother and some of her Spencer Club friends.

She was careful to establish a routine for her patient whose legs were still sore—so much walking, and so much rest. She found places in shops and parks for Mrs. Logan to sit down frequently.

They walked along Park Lane back to their hotel, and found mail and messages waiting for them. Cherry's mother had sent a second letter—the first was already there for her on the night of her arrival. Here was a letter from the Carewe Museum, saying stiffly that in view of Mrs. Logan's injury, her nurse would be admitted with her, as a very special exception. Peter Holt had telephoned and would try again. Archibald Hazard had telephoned inviting Mrs. Logan and Miss Ames to lunch the next day. Martha telephoned back and accepted. Then Cherry insisted on a long rest period.

"Can't we go to the theater this evening?" Martha asked. "It's that, or work on my notes."

"Now who's bullying whom?" Cherry said.

She ordered dinner in their rooms, went downstairs to the hotel lobby, and bought theater tickets and an evening newspaper. There was a story and photographs of the picturesque Shah and his recipes for good living. In his own hothouses he grew the flowers for his buttonhole. To stay healthy, the Shah recommended champagne every day. He couldn't be bothered with owning a car; when he needed one, he hired one, but had his own uniformed chauffeur. When he sang the school song at reunion dinners, tears ran down his beard.

Martha Logan was so amused, as Cherry read these eccentricities aloud to her during dinner, that she actually ate well for a change. They went on to the theater, and had a fine evening.

On Sunday at one o'clock they met Archibald Hazard at Simpson's in the Strand. In this formal, high-ceilinged restaurant with its large staff, Mr. Hazard looked small and eager. Cherry was sorry she could not like him better, since he was extending himself to entertain them. Martha Logan was glad to see him.

Once they were seated, they plunged into art talk. Cherry listened and learned, but she was diverted by the handsome people at other tables and by the excellent service and food. Mr. Hazard had ordered roast sirloin of beef and Yorkshire pudding. The roast was brought in on a trolley, and carved for them by a waiter.

"It deserves the lordly treatment," Mr. Hazard declared. "In each city I visit the very best restaurant serving roast beef. And believe me, Mrs. Logan, I am acquainted with the really fine restaurants of the world." He made an expansive gesture with his short, plump arms.

Cherry grinned at his fondness for roast beef. She did think he sounded like a phony, with all his pretentious talk, but she could be mistaken.

Now Mr. Hazard described the London art collections he had already visited. Martha Logan listened with interest.

"I'm going to see my friend, Pierre Selsam, at his gallery tomorrow afternoon," she said. "Poor Miss Cherry will have an overdose of paintings on this trip."

"Lucky Miss Cherry," said their host. He hesitated. "I haven't seen the show at the Selsam yet."

"Come along with us tomorrow," Martha invited. "I'm sure Pierre Selsam would be happy to meet you."

"Why, thanks," Mr. Hazard said. "I'd enjoy meeting him, and I'd enjoy seeing the exhibit in your company." They made arrangements for tomorrow.

When lunch was over, Mr. Hazard asked whether he could take them anywhere. Martha Logan explained that they were going now to visit some family friends of hers, in another part of London.

"If you'll just get a taxi for us, we'll appreciate it," Martha requested. She thanked him for a wonderful lunch. Cherry added her thanks, and followed her patient into the taxi.

They had not driven more than two blocks when Martha exclaimed, "That box of American nylon stockings I'm bringing my friends—I left it at the restaurant! I put it on the empty chair at our table and forgot it. How careless of me! Driver, take us back to Simpson's, please."

The taxi driver complied. As they pulled up in front of Simpson's, Cherry was surprised to see Mr. Hazard standing there deep in talk with a stocky, unshaven, roughly dressed man who might have been a mechanic or workman. What was striking was that the two men, so unlike, appeared to be on familiar terms. The workman was arguing with Mr. Hazard, who looked overbearing but was listening. As Cherry stepped out of the taxi, she had a good look at the muscular, dark-haired workman, and at Mr. Hazard's startled face when his eyes met Cherry's. Mr. Hazard raised his hat and came forward.

"Have you lost something, Miss Ames?" he asked. "May I help you? I'm obliged to speak to this man," Mr. Hazard said with some distaste, "but I can get rid of him if you or Mrs. Logan need me—"

Cherry thanked him and said No. Mr. Hazard raised his hat again, and both men walked off down the street.

In the restaurant Cherry recovered the package, and brought it back to Martha Logan. Her patient was sitting with her eyes closed. If she had seen Mr. Hazard and his companion, she did not remark on it. So Cherry let it go, and asked, "Are you in pain?"

"The arm aches a little, but it's not worth mentioning. No, I'm just resting." Cherry took her patient's word and did not offer medication. "Shall we go ahead now, driver?" Martha said.

A half hour's drive showed them many parts of London—much bigger than New York—with its many parks and tree-filled squares. Up a long hill, they arrived in a spacious neighborhood of houses and walled gardens.

Cherry thoroughly enjoyed the afternoon she spent with Martha Logan's friends in their garden. Such beautiful flowers! She had never seen such an abundance—nor such giant sweet peas, blooming in September at that—nor such glorious roses! Their hostess told her that flowers and trees thrived in England's mild, rainy climate, and gathered a bouquet for them. The children of the family took Cherry on a tour of the garden and introduced her to the bullfrog who lived in the little stream. Later in the afternoon, tea was served ceremoniously. Whenever Cherry thought of England after that, she remembered these kind people.

Monday afternoon Martha Logan and Cherry arrived at the Selsam Gallery to find Archibald Hazard already there, one of dozens of persons absorbed in the glowing paintings in the hushed, deeply carpeted rooms. Martha greeted him, and asked an attendant to tell Mr. Selsam that Mrs. Logan and two friends were here.

A very tall, thin, high-strung man quickly came out of an office. Pierre Selsam reminded Cherry of a greyhound.

"Martha! I *am* glad to see you! But what has happened to your arm?" Pierre Selsam asked, grasping her good left hand.

"A fall, just before I left. But it has provided me with this young nurse who is a delightful traveling companion. Miss Cherry Ames—" Mr. Selsam smiled and shook hands with Cherry, saying she must take the very best care of Mrs. Logan. Cherry smiled back. Martha said, "And this is Archibald Hazard. We met on the plane coming over."

The two men shook hands, Mr. Hazard saying how much he admired the exhibit. Cherry thought that next to Pierre Selsam, Mr. Hazard appeared much less impressive. She sensed something faintly false or insincere about pompous little Mr. Hazard. Martha Logan said, "How are you, Pierre?"

"Oh, splendid. Won't you come along to my office where we can have a chat?"

Cherry hung back, so that the two friends could visit in private. But Mr. Hazard marched right into the private office with them, so Cherry went along, too. Pierre Selsam drew up chairs for them, and asked Martha how her children were.

Her face lighted. "Bobby is shooting up like a bean sprout, and Ruth is turning into quite a young lady." They exchanged personal news for a few minutes. Mr. Hazard riffled through a catalogue with his left hand. He put it aside when Pierre Selsam said the exhibit was drawing record crowds.

"Marvelous show," Mr. Hazard said. "Finer than any I've seen in Paris or New York all year."

"Very kind of you to say so," Pierre Selsam said. "It's quite a responsibility, having nearly a million and a half dollars' worth of paintings on the premises. Of course the paintings are heavily insured."

"And of course you have a watchman," said Martha Logan.

"Oh, yes, I have a watchman patrol the alley all night, and the police make frequent rounds around the clock," Pierre Selsam said. "During the day I am here with the gallery caretaker, a guard, and the office staff. So I feel reasonably secure."

Mr. Hazard engaged the gallery owner in a discussion of the Renoirs, which he particularly admired. Cherry thought Mr. Hazard was being very careful in what little he said here this afternoon. The conversation turned to high-powered art investors who bought paintings as shrewdly as they would buy stocks and bonds to sell later on at higher prices. Pierre Selsam shook his head over collectors who cared nothing for art except to make a fortune out of trading in paintings.

Then he took his guests on a tour of the several rooms of the gallery, telling them anecdotes about some of the paintings. Cherry was dazzled by the colors and patterns. In the last room, someone knocked at a rear door. The guard unlocked and opened it to a deliveryman, whom he greeted by name and who handed him a carefully wrapped painting. Then the guard closed and locked the rear door again, and tried it to make sure it was locked. Pierre Selsam watched.

"I should think, sir," Mr. Hazard said, "that you would be as much concerned about any chance of fire as of theft."

"Indeed, yes. We did have a bit of trouble with a fire last year. That's why we installed a sprinkler system." Pierre Selsam pointed out this equipment, which was almost hidden from view. "Oh, I quite overlooked showing you this lovely Monet! Do you know how Monet came to paint this one?..."

It was a privileged visit. Finally Mrs. Logan said they must not take up any more of Pierre's time. When his three delighted visitors thanked him, Mr. Selsam said, "So happy to see you. Come back for another look some morning when there's less of a crowd here. Martha, shall I see you again this trip? You Americans are always in such a rush."

Martha Logan grinned, "I *can't* hurry in my present battered state. . . . Yes, do phone me."

She was limping with fatigue, Cherry noticed, as they left the art gallery. Cherry recommended that Martha take it easy the rest of the day, and on the following days space out her appointments to allow for periods of relaxation.

"What, no sightseeing?" she protested. "I always enjoy seeing the great sights over and over again. Not that I'd attempt walking through the Tower of London, or

Hampton Court Palace and gardens—you'll have to go by yourself, Cherry, while I'm resting or seeing the publisher or other people."

So, during the next few days, they followed this plan. Cherry appreciated Martha Logan's eagerness for her to see as much as possible, but took good care always to put her patient first. She kept watch to see that no swelling occurred in the right hand; if the cast on her right arm were proving too tight, it would constrict circulation and cause her right hand to swell. So far, so good. Cherry frequently changed the dressings on her patient's legs; the abrasions were healing slowly but satisfactorily.

On Wednesday she escorted her patient to the office of Dr. Alan Bates. It was two weeks since Mrs. Logan's accident—time to consult Dr. Bates, according to Dr. Merriam's instructions. Cherry learned that Dr. Bates was one of the topflight medical men in London. He had an assistant X-ray Mrs. Logan's arm; then the X-rays were developed, and the doctor looked at the film through a lighted view box. He said the arm was healing well, but the cast must remain. He also looked at the patient's bruised, scraped legs and was satisfied with their condition. Her general health seemed satisfactory.

"You're doing a good job, Nurse Ames," Dr. Bates said, then told both Cherry and Martha Logan, "You must have this arm X-rayed again in about two weeks. Where will you be then?" Edinburgh, they answered. "Capital, I shall refer you to an excellent physician there," Dr. Bates said.

He wrote out the name, Dr. Malcolm MacKenzie, and an address, with a note about his checkup of Mrs. Logan today. He handed these to Cherry.

"Dr. MacKenzie probably will remove the cast," he said. "In the meantime, Mrs. Logan, take care of yourself. See that she eats well, Nurse Ames, and rests sufficiently."

They thanked Dr. Bates and left his office.

Their week's stay in London was all too short. Martha Logan insisted she felt strong enough to take the peaceful boat ride along the Thames to Windsor Castle. Erected by William the Conqueror, and added to by other kings, the castle stood in the greenest countryside Cherry had ever seen. Once, while watching the changing of the guard at Buckingham Palace, they were caught in a sudden rain shower—but on the whole, the weather was perfect. By Friday, their last day in London, neither wanted to leave. They decided at breakfast to make the most of the day. Returning to Martha Logan's room for coats, they turned on the radio for a weather report. A news broadcast came on:

"—robbery at the Selsam Gallery last night," the announcer was saying. "The thieves stole thirty-five contemporary paintings valued at three hundred and fifty thousand pounds."

That was more than a million dollars. Mrs. Logan dropped her umbrella. She and Cherry stood motionless, listening.

"Police believe the thieves scaled the flat roofs of the area, bypassing the street and alley where a night watchman was on duty. The thieves forced open a rear door of the gallery, a fire-escape door, apparently using a small crowbar. They cut the paintings out of their frames, and left the empty frames on walls and floor.

"The robbery was discovered at seven o'clock this morning by the gallery caretaker, who comes in early to clean.

"The caretaker immediately called the police, and Scotland Yard is throwing out a massive dragnet for the thieves. Detectives are making an intensive search in the Mayfair area for clues. Ports and airports are being closely watched for the paintings, which, gallery owner Pierre Selsam believes, the thieves may try to smuggle immediately out of England to Russia or South America, to sell there. Interpol has been notified—"

"Poor Pierre!" Martha exclaimed.

The radio announcer went on. "The theft is one of the biggest and most daring ever staged in Britain. Mr. Selsam, interviewed within the hour, said the paintings were insured, but stressed that works of art are unique and irreplaceable. Mr. Selsam, profoundly shocked, pointed out that the theft was apparently masterminded by someone with a keen knowledge of art, who had selected only the finest works. Among the paintings stolen were—"

Martha Logan turned the radio off. "I don't want to hear any more," she said, and sat down, looking miserable. "My poor friend!" In a moment she remarked, "Well, I'm at least going to call Pierre."

She telephoned and told the gallery owner how shocked and sorry she was. After a short conversation she hung up.

"Pierre Selsam says," she told Cherry, "that the police do not suspect anyone in particular, so far. You know, hundreds of persons freely walk into an art gallery—the thieves could be anyone."

"No clues at all?" Cherry asked.

"None," Martha replied. "Can you imagine how shocked Mr. Hazard must be at this news? He greatly admired those Renoirs....That reminds me, I promised to call him up once more before we left. Would you mind putting the call through for me?"

"Not at all," Cherry said. She telephoned the Ritz, only to learn Archibald Hazard had checked out an hour ago. "Aren't you a little surprised he didn't phone you to say goodbye?" Cherry asked Mrs. Logan.

"No, the last time we saw him, Mr. Hazard told me he was rather busy," Martha replied. "It would have been a nice courtesy if he had phoned, but not necessary. We're just casual acquaintances."

The Selsam robbery left them feeling glum, but they went ahead with a morning of leisurely sightseeing. When they returned to their hotel, Cherry found she had again missed a telephone call from Peter Holt. This time he had left a message:

"Positively will see you in Stratford-upon-Avon next week!"

CHAPTER V

Cherry Meets Peter Again

CHERRY FELT ENCOURAGED. HER PATIENT SEEMED MUCH better on Saturday. She did not tire during the morning bus ride from London through rolling country to Oxford. In fact, she struck up lively conversations among the other American tourists who filled the bus. They said goodbye to their new acquaintances on reaching the ancient university town. Martha Logan had an appointment that afternoon with a scholar of English history, and research to do in the incomparable libraries.

Cherry escorted her from one medieval, formidable gray-stone building to another, and took notes for her. On the way they had glimpses of chapels, stone arcades, gardens, and bell towers. A few masters and students were here early, before the school term started. That evening Cherry and Martha dined on beefsteak stew, pickled walnuts, and Queen's pudding, and slept that night in high-ceilinged old bedrooms. Next morning they attended a formal Sunday church service, then lunched and boarded a bus for Stratford-upon-Avon.

Nearing Stratford they saw, at a distance, several brightly dressed young persons on bicycles. Cherry wondered if they might be Peter Holt's students.

Cherry fell in love on sight with Shakespeare's little town, deep in the country. Their bus drove beside the gentle River Avon, where swans glided under willow trees. As the bus turned onto cobblestoned High Street, Cherry exclaimed, "Why, this is just a pleasant country town!" Its rows of Tudor half-timbered brick and plaster houses, with their latticed windows and flowering window boxes, looked inviting and homelike.

Martha smiled at Cherry's delight. "If Will Shakespeare were to come back," she said, "he'd find his town little changed."

They alighted from the bus at one of the two or three big inns in Stratford. Cherry registered for her patient and herself, and was seeing about their luggage when someone said:

"Oh, there you are! I figured that any day now you'd turn up either at the Falcon Inn or the Welcombe or here. I've been inquiring at all of them."

Cherry turned and saw Peter Holt, looking delighted and sunburned. He wore tennis clothes and carried a racket. He pumped Cherry's hand, greeted Martha Logan, and invited them to have tea with him right now, all in one breath. Cherry was pleased to see him again—and knew she must be showing it; otherwise, why did Martha look so amused? Martha said: "Why don't you two have tea together? I'll just go up to my room and work on my notes." But Peter persuaded her to come along, and escorted them to a tearoom next door to the inn.

They had just sat down, and were deciding on orange squash instead of hot tea, when a very tall, very thin, fair young man in tennis clothes stopped at their table.

"I say, Holt, I've nothing against your looking for this girl, as girls go," he said cheerfully, "but have you quite forgotten the sterling character with whom you have a tennis date? I refer, naturally, to myself."

Cherry's mouth opened at the sight of this tall, limp young man, who reminded her of an earthworm standing on end. Martha Logan's face said plainly: *"Who in the world is this?"*

"Oh, I am sorry, Ryder," said Peter, getting up. "You wandered off there, and then when I found my friends—" He apologized and asked Ryder to join them, signaling the waitress for a fourth orange squash.

Ryder stood jauntily before them, plucking at his tennis racket as if it were a banjo. "I was about to suggest another game, but instinct tells me you won't bob up on the court again today. Ladies"—Ryder bowed a little to them—"I was advising Holt on his backhand drive, and he was advising me on Shakespeare."

"Sit down, Ryder," Peter said with a grin. "Rodney Ryder has taken a sudden interest in Shakespeare."

Ryder sat down, folding his lean length to cramp himself into the chair. His eyes were like blue icicles, and Cherry noticed he had a habit of blinking.

"My dear fellow," Ryder said, "why shouldn't I fancy going along with your learned little band to the Shakespeare exhibit again tomorrow?" He gave the two ladies a bland smile.

Peter hid his amusement. "Certainly, come along, if you like. Mrs. Logan, Miss Cherry Ames, this is Mr. Ryder."

Rodney Ryder's expression changed as the American made the introductions. He looked uncomfortable. Perhaps, Cherry thought, Ryder knew of Martha Logan's reputation as a writer, and felt self-conscious at finding himself in the company of the well-known historical novelist. Ryder blinked rapidly, said, "How d'you do? So happy to meet you. Now I must trot along and—er—telephone."

"Here come our refreshments—" Peter put a detaining hand on the other young man's arm. But Ryder clambered to his feet, mumbling, "Tennis tomorrow, at two on the tick? And then off for more Shakespeare?"

"It's a date," Peter agreed. "Before you go, you've got to recite that toast you said for us yesterday. Please."

Rodney Ryder lifted his glass and reeled off, as fast as he could:

> *"Here's to you as good as you are*
> *And here's to me as bad as I am*
> *And as bad as I am, and as good as you are,*
> *I'm as good as you are as bad as I am."*

He took one gulp of his orange squash, said good-bye, and shot out of the tearoom.

"What an extraordinary young man!" Martha said, and the three of them exploded with pent-up laughter.

"Why did he run away from us like that?" Cherry wanted to know. Peter shrugged.

Martha Logan asked, "Is he genuinely interested in Shakespeare?"

"Well, Ryder tags along with us to exhibits and asks questions," Peter said. He explained that when he and his students arrived in Stratford on Friday afternoon, Rodney Ryder was wandering around looking for a tennis partner. "He saw me carrying a racket, and that was the beginning of our constant companionship. Ryder certainly is giving me a rush," Peter said, a little ruefully. "I told him I'm here to teach, and to learn, too—that my students and I would be busy, really busy. I'm fortunate enough to have a letter through a university contact to a Shakespeare curator who's here in charge of a special exhibit. But Rodney Ryder is not a man you can discourage easily." Peter smiled and shook his head. "I guess he really *is* interested. He seems fairly well educated, nice manners, probably quite bright if and when he's ever serious. Anyway, Ryder plays a good game of tennis, and my students think he's entertaining company."

Martha Logan asked, "What does your learned curator make of your Rodney Ryder?"

"They haven't met yet, and frankly I can't visualize such a meeting," Peter said. "By the way, you two mustn't miss seeing the paintings of characters from the Shakespearean plays."

"Oh, yes, the London newspapers have been full of news of this exhibit for weeks," Martha said. "Well, we'll be in Stratford for several days, so there's no hurry."

"Tomorrow is the last day to see it," Peter said. "After tomorrow, the paintings will be shipped to Edinburgh to go on public exhibit there."

They were all going on to Edinburgh, but agreed it would be more appropriate to see the Shakespearean paintings here. Peter invited Martha and Cherry to come along the next afternoon, with his students "and probably with Rodney Ryder," to see the paintings and meet the curator.

They compared notes for a while on what they had seen and done in London. Mention of the art museums reminded Peter of Archibald Hazard. "He's awfully knowledgeable about paintings, isn't he?"

Martha Logan answered, "I rather thought so, too, on the plane. But do you know, I've been thinking, and I've changed my mind about him. I wonder if he isn't bluffing some of his knowledge. Oh, Mr. Hazard knows the main facts, and he knows the financial value of paintings, but that's about all."

Cherry was interested to hear Martha confirm her own impression—that Mr. Hazard might be rather a phony. Not that it mattered, they'd probably never see Mr. Hazard again.

Their glasses of orange squash were emptied, and Cherry thought Martha Logan looked tired. As they rose to go to their rooms, thanking Peter, he asked, "Who would like to go for a walk this evening?"

"Cherry is a great walker," Martha said with a straight face. "As for me, I plan to work on my notes this evening....Yes, Nurse Ames, I promise to go to bed early."

So, after dinner, Cherry found herself strolling along the riverbank with Peter. She enjoyed the country quiet, and the clear, sweet air, and the snatches of Shakespeare that Peter recited for her. His choices all were so romantic that she giggled.

"What's funny," he demanded, "about 'Lady, by yonder blessed moon I swear, That tips with silver all these fruit-tree tops—'?"

"I'm sorry," Cherry said. "I've had such matter-of-fact training in the sciences that I guess I don't have your appreciation of poetry."

"That's no reason why we can't be friends, and good friends, is it?" Peter said. "I have to confess to you that I flunked biology *twice*."

Cherry laughed. "Wouldn't it be a dull world if we were all alike?"

"I like you," Peter announced, and took her hand as they walked. He told her about his students, whom he was fond of. They all were staying at a small pension in Stratford. Later in the week they planned to rent bicycles, and cycle part of the way to Edinburgh.

"You really see the country from a bicycle," Peter said. "We stop and study along the way, of course—otherwise, the kids wouldn't get university credit for

this study tour. Yesterday we cycled over to see War-
wick Castle. Good hiking around here, too. For a start
you and I could stroll out to see Anne Hathaway's
cottage and garden. She was Mrs. Shakespeare, you
know. I should say, Mistress Shakespeare. Anyway, it's
not far, and you like to walk."

Cherry was about to say she walked miles on hospital duty, that on a trip she'd prefer a bicycle or even a
ride on the handlebars of his bicycle, when a laughing
crowd of young people appeared at a bend in the lane.

"There's Mr. Holt!" a boy cried out. "We've been looking for you!" A girl called out, "We thought you might
be with Rodney Ryder."

"Not exactly," Peter said to Cherry under his
breath.

His students emerged from leafy shadows into bright
moonlight, and surrounded them. Peter did not appear
much older than these boys and girls in their late teens.
He introduced them to Cherry—a brother and sister
from a ranch, Douglas and Deborah Kimball; Nancy
Cerutti, who came from St. Louis; quiet, big Ken Eck-
lund; Mary McBride who was animatedly explaining
something to Masakiyo Yamonoto, a classmate and an
exchange student from Japan, and several other lively
students. Cherry liked them all, and liked the respect
and affection they showed to Peter. But romance was
over for the evening, as they all walked back to the inn.

Next day Martha, too, eventually met Peter's students. She and Cherry made morning visits to Shakespeare's church, and to the thatch-roofed cottage where

the poet and his wife Anne and their children had lived. The cottage still held its crude wooden settles and cradles, its pewter vessels and candlesticks at the fireplaces. The goose-feather beds were still made with lavender-scented flax sheets. After a rest in the hedge-walled garden, Cherry insisted on a leisurely lunch and on her patient's necessary nap. Then they went downstairs to the lobby of the inn, where students swarmed around them, and they were off to the exhibit of paintings, with Peter in the lead.

Martha Logan disengaged herself from the admiring students and asked, "Where is Mr. Ryder?"

Peter, still flushed from tennis, said, "I think Rodney Ryder is shy of you, ma'am. At any rate, he said he'd 'pop up to meet the curator after I've been a bit mellowed with food.' Guess Ryder wanted a bite first."

"What is he doing in Stratford, of all unlikely places to find that frivolous character?" Cherry asked.

"Says he's on vacation and wants to soak up culture," Peter answered. "He seems to have plenty of leisure and money. I tried asking Ryder what he does, but he said 'Don't be idiotic, my dear chap, I have no talent for work.'"

Everyone laughed, and someone said, "Rodney's a lot of fun."

At one of the larger houses they went in and waited while Peter sought out the curator, Philip Lawrence. Waiting, they looked at the extraordinary collection of paintings temporarily hung in these rooms. Here were King Lear, Macbeth, Ophelia, and Caesar, here a brooding Hamlet looked out of the frame, and here were the English kings and jesters and ladies of Shakespeare's plays.

Martha Logan said in delight, "Look, some of these are portraits of the great Shakespearean actors of the past. And look at this murky old picture! Why, these paintings must cover a span of three or four hundred years." She agreed with the students that the curator had brought together a marvelous collection. "I've heard of Mr. Lawrence," Martha said, "though I've never had the privilege of meeting him. He's widely known as an Elizabethan scholar, a very able man."

Mr. Lawrence came out with Peter, to meet the American writer and her companion, and Peter's students. The curator was a gentle, dignified, gray-haired man, eager to tell his visitors all he could.

"This collection is unique, I believe," Mr. Lawrence said, "in that the paintings have come from all over England, some from other countries. Everything here is on loan from museums and universities and private owners. It's most unusual to have so comprehensive—so rare—a Shakespeare display assembled all in one place at one time."

Peter, Martha Logan, and the students had a great many questions. Mr. Lawrence obligingly answered all of them. Cherry listened, enjoying the pictures, and half looking for Rodney Ryder who amused her so much. He did not come. Ryder did not show up for tea later. Peter remarked, "He knew where we'd be all afternoon. Well, I guess Ryder latched onto another tennis partner."

"Someone who can teach him about Shakespeare while batting a tennis ball?" Martha joked.

"Perhaps that *is* my fascination for him," Peter said. "He's pinned me down to a regular tennis date for every day we're here."

"You," Cherry said gently to Martha, "have a date any minute now to rest.... Yes, you do. Particularly if we're to go to the Shakespeare Memorial Theater this evening." This was like offering a carrot to a rabbit.

Martha Logan made a sweeping theatrical gesture. "Sweet nurse, let us away. To you, my good lord Peter, and young friends all"—she stood up grandly—"I must begone. Mistress Cherry hath decreed it. Adieu."

Peter and his students rose too. "'Parting is such sweet sorrow,'" said Peter, and doffed an imaginary plumed hat.

Between the acts that evening, they all met on the theater's outdoor promenade beside the river. Peter obviously wanted to speak to Cherry alone, but had no chance. And next day they all met briefly again, in the sunny meadows outside the town, where ferns and blackberries grew near the streams. Peter and his students and Rodney Ryder had bicycled out for a picnic. Ryder, trying to catch a cow, stumbled all over his long, lean self. Everybody watched in amusement as the cow triumphed and got away. Cherry was sorry when Martha Logan, after a few minutes, declined Peter's invitation to join the picnic and instructed their taxi driver to drive them on. Later that day Peter came by their hotel, and returned in the evening, but

Cherry was not free to see him, except for a moment each time.

"No, Mrs. Logan isn't sick," Cherry answered Peter's question. "In fact, she's regaining her strength in this country air. But she has to work on her research notes for her next book. I help her, you see."

Peter understood about working hard and systematically on these trips. "Tomorrow, then?" he asked Cherry. "Right after my tennis date with Ryder? We could spend most of the afternoon together."

Cherry smiled. "I think you're as mad about tennis as Rodney Ryder is. Are all college instructors as athletic as you?"

Peter ignored her teasing. "Please come. We're leaving late tomorrow afternoon, darn it. Come and watch me play. Two on the tick, at the tennis courts?"

Cherry promised to try to arrange for time off. Of course her amiable employer said Yes. On the following day, Wednesday, Cherry arrived a little after two, to find Peter alone on one of the grass courts.

"Hi, Peter!" said Cherry. "Where's Rodney Ryder?"

"He hasn't showed up yet. I'm annoyed with him for another reason, too. Am I glad to see you!"

"Is that a compliment, or do you just see me as a substitute tennis partner?" Cherry asked with a grin.

"Compliment," Peter said. "Let's sit at that table under the umbrella while we wait for him. I have something to tell you." He smiled at her as they sat down together. "You're so pretty. I'll bet you look wonderful in a nurse's uniform, all in white."

"Thank you," Cherry said, smiling back at him. "Now what's on the Holt mind?"

"Well, I saw Mr. Lawrence this morning, and he told me that Rodney Ryder came in alone to see him late Monday afternoon—after we left the exhibit hall. Ryder introduced himself as a friend of mine, and somehow gave Mr. Lawrence the impression that he's one of our student group." Peter frowned. "I feel Ryder took rather a liberty. He never mentioned his visit to me, either, unless he forgot. What bothers me is that he asked the curator so many questions."

"What sort of questions?" Cherry asked. "Mr. Lawrence is so gracious, I suppose he answered Ryder's questions?"

"Well, he answered within limits. Mr. Lawrence didn't know whether to think Rodney Ryder is simply foolish and ignorant, or else inordinately inquisitive. The point is, though, that Ryder had no right to impose on the curator for a private interview without my knowledge. Ryder *knew* we were all going to have tea at that hour on Monday afternoon, and where—he could have joined us and asked me to introduce him to the curator."

"Or Rodney Ryder could have come when we all went to meet the curator," Cherry said. "Hmm. Did Ryder have any special reason for wanting to talk with Mr. Lawrence privately?"

"I can't imagine any sensible reason," Peter said. "Oh, he's just scatterbrained—just wandered to the exhibit an hour late, and went rambling on to the curator the way he's been throwing aimless questions at me. Ryder probably has no idea that one shouldn't waste the time of a distinguished scholar in that irresponsible way."

Cherry remarked that it was silly of Ryder to be so impressed and intimidated by Martha Logan that he ran away, but all boldness with the eminent Philip Lawrence. "Unless he's plain ignorant about Mr. Lawrence, or is scared of women. What sort of questions did he ask Mr. Lawrence?" Cherry asked again.

"Perfectly innocent questions," Peter replied. "Which paintings of the Shakespearean characters are the most famous, which the rarest, or the oldest." Peter grinned ruefully. "Poor Mr. Lawrence! I apologized to him all over the place. I'm going to give Ryder a good bawling out if it will register with that featherbrain." Peter looked at his wristwatch. "He's twenty minutes late for our tennis date. Come on. Let's go to his inn and see if we can find him. I lent him my book of Shakespeare's plays, and he promised to return it today."

Peter left word with an attendant at the tennis court, in case Ryder showed up. Then he and Cherry started out for Ryder's inn, along cobblestoned High Street. Ryder would come along High Street, Peter said, if he were heading for the tennis courts. But they did not see his tall, skinny, apparently boneless figure. They passed the exhibit hall, and Cherry said, "I'd like to see those paintings again."

"You'll have to wait and see them when you get to Edinburgh," Peter said. "Mr. Lawrence and his staff packed them up all day yesterday, and this morning they were put on the train to Edinburgh."

"Accompanied by a guard, I hope," Cherry said.

"Yes, certainly. They're all catalogued and insured." Peter guffawed. "Ryder actually offered to help Mr. Lawrence pack the paintings. In his enthusiasm for all things Shakespearean! He only means to be amiable and helpful, but can you imagine! He'd put his big feet through two or three of the canvases while he was 'helping.'"

Cherry laughed. "He'll probably forget all about Shakespeare the moment he's left Stratford."

At the small inn where Rodney Ryder was staying, Peter and Cherry went to the desk. They asked the pleasant, pink-cheeked woman in charge whether Mr. Ryder was in.

"I believe Mr. Ryder left last evening," the woman said. She glanced at the inn's account books. "Yes, he has gone."

Peter stared. "I mean *Rodney* Ryder—a tall, thin young man—blinks his eyes rapidly—joking, light-hearted—"

"Yes, I mean the tall, thin Mr. Ryder who blinks," the woman said, "although he impressed me as being quite serious and preoccupied."

It was Cherry's turn to stare. "I never saw Ryder serious about anything, the few times we met—not even about Shakespeare," she said.

The woman asked, "Are we talking about the same person? Our Mr. Ryder was *most* silent and reserved.

Oh, yes, he did have one discussion with my husband, about cricket, rugby, soccer, and tennis."

"That's our man," said Peter, baffled. "Did Mr. Ryder leave any message?"

The woman glanced into a file. "Sorry, sir, there's nothing.... Oh, yes. Are you Mr. Holt? He left this book for you." Peter thanked the woman. She hesitated. "Mr. Ryder left rather in haste last evening, after he made a long-distance telephone call. Possibly an emergency—?"

"Possibly," said Peter. "Well—thank you very much." He and Cherry went outdoors. "If that isn't just like that unreliable character! I hope he wasn't called home by some drastic emergency."

"And so farewell to Rodney Ryder," said Cherry. "But I don't understand—how come he gave the people at the inn such a different impression than the one he gave us? Or did he naturally react like that to your lively young students?"

Peter shrugged. The question did not interest him. What concerned him now was the fact that he and his students were leaving Stratford late tomorrow afternoon, on their bicycles, and between then and now he had people to see and arrangements to make.

"So this is my last hour with you," Peter said.

"You sound like a condemned man," Cherry said, laughing.

"I ought to answer something witty and touching," Peter said, "but the best I can think of is that I want to see you again. When will you and Mrs. Logan be in Edinburgh?"

"In about a week—" Cherry opened her handbag and consulted her itinerary, tucked in her passport, which she always carried. She told Peter the exact dates for their Edinburgh stay, and the name of their hotel.

"Fine!" he said, brightening. "We'll be there around the same time, and we're booked at the same hotel. But"—his intelligent face changed expression—"after Edinburgh, what? You live in Illinois and I live in Oregon. Two thousand miles apart. From the Mississippi River to the Pacific Ocean. Well, there are jet planes."

"We could always meet here in England, where the distances aren't so great," Cherry suggested teasingly.

"A perfect idea," Peter said. "Let's go for a walk," and he started to sing a song about "the foggy, foggy dew."

Along the way, as they walked, he gathered wildflowers for Cherry. At one place she insisted he was helping himself to late roses off somebody's garden wall, but he declared gallantly:

"You deserve roses. They match the roses in your cheeks. Now, isn't that poetic, Miss Nurse?"

"My rosy cheeks indicate a preponderance of red corpuscles in my bloodstream, and a lack of any biochemical trace of anemia," Cherry replied. "Shall I translate?"

He laughed and said, *"That* distance between us isn't so great." When they turned back and reached her inn, Peter presented her with the bouquet. "Tell Mrs. Logan this one"—he touched a pink-and-white flower—"is the York and Lancaster rose. And tell her goodbye for me. See you next week, Cherry."

Peter kissed her on the cheek. Cherry was so surprised that she went upstairs to the wrong floor.

She missed Peter that moonlit evening, an ideal evening for a country stroll. But she and Martha Logan were leaving tomorrow themselves; there were notes and packing to do, and Cherry made another routine, but careful, checkup of her patient. As eight thirty approached, Martha said, "Oh, why waste an evening on chores? We're in Stratford, and they're playing *Romeo and Juliet* tonight! Come on, Cherry, we'll finish these little jobs later—"

"I can see you're feeling much better!" Cherry snatched up a coat for Martha Logan and followed her, almost running.

They arrived puffing at the theater in time to see the curtain go up.

CHAPTER VI

A Fantastic Visitor

THE NEXT FEW DAYS WERE STRENUOUS—AND FULL OF discovery for Cherry. She and Martha Logan again boarded a tour bus, leaving behind the sunny orchards and hay barns to travel northeast through the Midlands, into busy manufacturing and market towns of great age. The weather grew colder in this high north country. In Chester they walked briskly around the Roman wall, and shopped in the medieval Rows, for antique silver that Martha loved. She regretted that they had to travel so fast and were getting only glimpses of England.

They traveled farther north into hills and green forests and the calm blue waters of the Lake District. The mid-September weather grew still colder, sometimes rainy. They wore coats, and Cherry tucked woolen lap robes around her patient and herself in the bus. They were grateful for hot baked apples with custard and steaming tea when they arrived at Windermere late Saturday afternoon.

They were to stay for three nights at this rambling old wooden country hotel beside a lake. The Carewe Museum was in this area, forty miles from the hotel. The hotel manager said he would engage a local taximan to drive them there; after a day's rest they would visit the private museum.

Cherry was concerned that Martha might have grown overtired. That Saturday evening the most Cherry would allow her patient to do, after dinner, was to watch television in one of the hotel's public sitting rooms. After a newscast, white-bearded Shah Liddy came on the screen and gave another interview. Martha Logan was diverted by his bristling white eyebrows, white beard, and extravagant mannerisms. She was so amused she scarcely noticed that it was only nine o'clock when her nurse shooed her to bed.

Their day of rest fell, appropriately, on Sunday. The sun shone, and it was a joy to be deep in the country this autumn day.

"Let's walk to the village," Martha said eagerly to Cherry. "The Lake District is a hiker's paradise, you know."

"Aren't you being awfully ambitious?" Cherry asked. She knew that her patient's bruised legs were nearly healed by now, and Mrs. Logan had recovered from the shock of the fall—but her general health still lagged. "We've already done quite a lot of traveling and sightseeing on the way up here," Cherry cautioned her. "What about a drive today, or just a short walk?"

"Oh, I'm fine!" Martha Logan made an impatient, clumsy gesture with her right arm in its cast. "Besides, it's a perfectly beautiful day!"

Cherry reluctantly gave in. A walk in this bracing air might do her patient good. The village was not very far away, along a road that rose to cut through forests, and dipped beside meadows. One thing struck Cherry as they walked—on either side of them, tall, thick hedges enclosed the meadows, high stone walls guarded the privacy of gardens. At times she and Martha were walled in on the road, unable to see anything except treetops and the unwinding ribbon of road straight ahead.

"We don't usually have walls, or walls of hedges, at home," Cherry said uncomfortably. "I guess I'm used to 'the great wide open spaces.'"

"Well, we have immense lands and a relatively small population per square mile, outside the cities," Martha Logan said. "For a long time, while our wild new, young country was being settled, parts of it had no population, except for Indian tribes, and one or two lonely settlers. It was a rare event when a traveler or a new settler came by—people were glad to see him, and gave him food and lodging and helped him. That's how it happens that Americans are generally very friendly. With Europeans, who have smaller countries and dense populations, living close together, they're inclined to be more cautious and reserved.

Also, they're much older peoples than we are, more sophisticated—" Martha Logan smiled. "Our differences can enrich one another. The main thing is for us to get better acquainted."

They came to an open view. Martha's serious expression turned joyful. "Oh, look at that lake with the sun on it!" She recited a snatch of a poem, then broke off. "This is Wordsworth country, Cherry."

Cherry obliged by chanting, "'I wandered lonely as a cloud, That floats on high o'er vales and hills...' Anyway, I can't help wondering what goes on behind these walls and high hedges."

"Wait until tomorrow. We'll go behind the walls of the Carewe estate. Ah—you know, Cherry—I do feel a little tired."

They turned back without ever reaching the village. Cherry insisted Mrs. Logan rest in bed for the greater part of the day "and eat all the nourishing food you can hold."

Martha Logan grinned. "For once I won't argue with you. Tomorrow is the big day."

A maid knocked on the door of Martha Logan's room Monday morning. "The taxi you ordered is waiting for you, ma'am."

Cherry, putting on her coat in the adjoining room, heard Martha call out, "Thank you. We'll be right down." Her voice sounded tired.

Cherry rapped, went in, and said, "If you aren't feeling too well, do you have to go to the Carewe

Museum this morning? Couldn't you telephone and ask whether you could come tomorrow?"

"Of course I must go this morning! You've heard how fussy the Carewe Museum people are about appointments. I feel perfectly well, just not very energetic."

Well, they had crossed an ocean to keep this appointment, so difficult to get in the first place. Cherry decided she had no reason to worry, provided her patient did not overdo today. She escorted Martha Logan down the hotel's wide staircase and out into the courtyard.

A chunky, fair-haired man in a rumpled suit and chauffeur's cap—a local man—came up to Mrs. Logan and said, "Good morning, ma'am, at your service." He looked pleasant and responsible. Mrs. Logan asked him his name. It was Edwin. He said he could give them as much of his time today as they might need. He led them to an old, well-kept sedan and helped them in.

During the leisurely drive to the Carewe estate, Edwin was closemouthed. He did point out a few sights, and when Mrs. Logan ventured to ask him, said he had lived in this part of England all his life, and he and his wife had six children. Cherry thought, in amusement, how an American taxi driver, if he were driving foreigners through his own part of the country, would regale them with local history and anecdotes, and would ask the visitors questions about their country. But Martha Logan was silent, too—probably thinking about what she most wanted to see at the

Carewe collection in relation to her book. Cherry kept quiet, enjoying the countryside and occasional villages they were driving through. The roads were nearly deserted. Only a public bus or two and a few farm wagons passed along these hilly roads.

Punctually at ten o'clock they arrived at the Carewe estate, which was enclosed by a high stone wall. At the gate a guard inspected their letters of admission. Edwin was permitted to drive his passengers up the short roadway to the stone mansion and to park there, with the understanding that he remain in or near his taxi, within sight of the gate guard. Cherry noticed another guard patrolling the grounds outside the mansion.

"The house is smaller than I'd expected," Martha murmured to Cherry as they rang and waited at the carved double doors. "Small and elegant."

"Does Mr. Carewe live here?" Cherry asked.

"No, this is now a museum, not a residence. I believe Mr. Carewe lives in a newer house on another part of this estate—when he's here at all."

The door opened, and a woman in brown with her hair severely pulled back admitted them. Martha Logan introduced herself and Cherry.

"Come in. You are expected," the woman said. Her voice was clipped and precise. "I am Miss Hayden, Mr. Carewe's secretary. Will you wait in the library? Mr. Carewe will see you in a few minutes."

They stepped in. Martha looked faintly surprised. "I hadn't known we were to have the privilege of meeting Mr. Carewe."

"Mr. Carewe makes a point of meeting visitors to his collection," the secretary said. Her voice held overtones, suggesting the great collector's fondness for these particular paintings, and his critical attitude toward the few visitors he chose to let see them. Cherry felt the intimacy of the place, even as she glimpsed a guard in a room beyond.

Miss Hayden led them through a marble foyer hung with pictures and into a library. Here, at a long table littered with books and papers, another woman was working. She was plump, untidy, and jolly looking behind her heavy glasses.

"This is Mrs. Ogilvie, our librarian and scholar, who catalogued the collection," said the secretary. "Mrs. Logan, and her nurse, Miss Ames."

They all said, "How do you do?" The librarian invited them to sit down, regretting that there was no couch, only some antique and very hard wooden chairs.

"Are you the curator, too, Mrs. Ogilvie?" Martha Logan asked.

"Oh, dear, no," the librarian said cheerfully. "Mr. Carewe is his own curator. When he is away, as he often is, Mr. Patwell is in charge. Mr. Patwell doesn't often have a holiday, I can tell you. Today is one of his rare ones. Wouldn't you like a catalogue?" She gave them each one, and they thanked her.

Cherry could see into an adjoining office, where the secretary was talking with a tall, rawboned spare man, wearing an easy-fitting, worn tweed jacket. He turned around, and Cherry saw his face was a spider's web of wrinkles, and his hair ash white. John Carewe must be a very old man.

He came in with the secretary, and regarded the two visitors quizzically while Miss Hayden introduced them. He shook their hands.

"It's kind of you to let us come," Martha Logan said to him. "It's especially kind of you to make an exception on short notice for Miss Ames."

Mr. Carewe nodded and said, "Happy to have you," in an indifferent tone. Something about him made Cherry think of a giant whose strength was spent. He complimented Martha Logan on her work and asked a question or two about the book for which she was doing research. As she answered, his eyes grew sharp and bright.

"Then the portraits here should interest you very particularly, Mrs. Logan," he said. "May I have the pleasure of showing you some of them?"

With a slight gesture he led them out of the library, through the foyer again, and into a room hung with paintings. Apparently once a drawing room, it still held a few fine chairs and small rugs on the parquet floor. Mr. Carewe took them around the room and Cherry saw another lovely room beyond.

Mr. Carewe said, "This is a famous Reynolds portrait, as you know." They paused to admire it. "This Romney—which I myself think even finer—has a unique historical interest." He began telling them about the lady in the portrait.

"Cherry, will you please take notes?" Martha Logan whispered. "This stupid cast—" she half apologized to Mr. Carewe.

He nodded and finished his story. Then he said, "Perhaps now you would like to be free to browse by yourselves? Most visitors prefer to do that. You'll find the paintings are displayed in ten rooms, and there are two floors. If you have any questions, I or my staff will be happy to try to answer them."

Martha Logan started to thank him, but was cut short by voices and some confusion at the entrance door. Miss Hayden came in with a look of suppressed excitement. She said in a low voice to Mr. Carewe:

"I beg your pardon—unexpected visitors, Mr. Carewe —the Shah and Lady Liddy. They've motored up from a friend's country place, although they haven't ever applied for admission. They're hoping you might just receive them." She looked overwhelmed.

"The Shah! Indeed," said the old collector. Cherry could not interpret his sudden change of expression. He glanced at his watch, remarking that it was ten fifteen and he wanted no visitors after twelve. "Well, at the very least we mustn't keep them standing on the doorstep, must we? If you will excuse me, Mrs. Logan, Miss Ames—"

He and the secretary went into the foyer where the door stood open. Cherry and Martha frankly watched and listened. The Shah was every bit as theatrical looking as on television, and a great deal more forceful when seen in person. His presence was like a strong wind blowing on all of them. His voice boomed out and his white beard waggled as he announced:

"My dear Mr. Carewe, I realize this is a frightful imposition! If time weren't running out for us on this trip, I shouldn't be throwing myself on your kindness in this way. But I *can't* leave England—not knowing when either you or I shall be back again—without seeing one of the last great, privately held art collections in the world! Do, I beg you, let us see your fabled treasures!"

Cherry noticed that John Carewe looked flattered. Lady Liddy, a delicate-looking blond young woman in a wide-brimmed hat, luxurious suit and furs, entreated him, too.

Cherry missed Mr. Carewe's reply as Martha Logan spoke under her breath. "The world's great personages and the leading art scholars come here—the Shah is celebrated on both counts. How can Mr. Carewe possibly refuse him?"

John Carewe hesitated only a second or two. He bowed to Lady Liddy, then extended his hand to the millionaire art patron, saying in his dry, tired way, "This is an unexpected pleasure for me—a great pleasure to meet you. Come in, come in. Miss Hayden," he instructed the secretary, "will you kindly tell the Shah's chauffeur to be ready for them at twelve?"

Through the window Cherry saw an imposing black car and a uniformed chauffeur waiting. Miss Hayden went out to speak to him, while the Shah made a deprecating remark about his rented car. "However, it's my usual practice to rent cars, so much less nuisance than dragging along one's own car across the Continent. But of course we bring our own reliable chauffeur."

"Quite," said Mr. Carewe. "Lady Liddy, would you and your husband be good enough to sign my guest book?"

At this, Martha Logan grinned at Cherry. He hadn't asked *them* to sign. John Carewe called out, "Mrs. Ogilvie! We require two catalogues for our distinguished guests." The librarian bustled out with the catalogues as Mr. Carewe had the imposing Shah and his young wife sign the register. The Shah complained that he felt the cold, being accustomed to the hot weather of the Near East.

"I hope you'll forgive my unsightliness, Mr. Carewe, if I keep my mackintosh over my shoulders," the Shah said.

The lightweight waterproof topcoat flapped around his short, round figure like the slack sails of a ship, and Cherry held back a smile.

Then Mr. Carewe ushered them into the first room where Cherry and Martha stood. Cherry realized she was staring. She turned away to study the paintings, as Martha Logan did. But she could not resist stealing glances at the short, rotund Shah with the perfect rose in his buttonhole. His young wife hovered nearby, quiet and self-effacing. He riffled through the catalogue, using his left hand, and remarked—arrogantly, Cherry thought—that the hanging of the paintings was "rather well done."

Mr. Carewe said, "I asked the advice of the curator of the National Gallery. He helped me work out how to display the collection." It was said modestly, and was not lost on the Shah who launched into an informed comparison of the collections at London's National and Tate galleries with this collection.

John Carewe was impressed. He asked the Shah about his own collection of paintings. The Shah charmingly declined to talk about his own treasures. "Not here, my dear Mr. Carewe, where one is in such close touch with so many masterpieces! Just let me enjoy *your* treasures."

"I see you will not need my services as a guide," Mr. Carewe said to the Shah. "Please feel free to look around by yourselves. I shall be interested to learn what you and Lady Liddy think."

As he had told the Americans, he told the Shah and his wife that there were ten rooms, two floors. He did not introduce the two sets of visitors, since there was no reason to. They politely ignored one another as Mr. Carewe left the four of them alone together.

Martha Logan had finished viewing the first room, and now moved into the second room. Cherry followed her. For a while they took notes on the paintings of the famous Henry and the two sisters. Lady Mary did wear the fabled ring for her portrait, Mrs. Logan was glad to see. The Shah came in, gave the Americans a pleasant glance, and planted himself before a great canvas with his back to them. Young Lady Liddy drifted through the second room, and went into the third by herself.

The minutes slowly went by as the visitors sometimes passed one another, sometimes missed one another in various rooms. The mansion, though relatively small, had a number of stairways, landings, and passageways in which it was easy to lose sight of one another. For a few minutes during their tour of the rooms Cherry "lost" Martha. She hunted up one of the two indoor guards who directed her to her patient.

By the time Cherry and Martha Logan had seen most of the paintings on the second floor, Cherry felt concerned that her patient was growing overtired. Standing and walking in a gallery was very tiring, and Martha drooped.

"Don't you think you've done enough?" Cherry asked. "You mustn't let yourself become exhausted."

"I *am* tired, but it's only a little after eleven," Martha protested. "I don't want to cut our visit short."

"Well, if you'd sit down and rest for a few minutes—"

A guard hurried in, "Is one of you ladies a nurse?" he asked.

"I'm a nurse," said Cherry. "What happened?"

"If you could come downstairs directly, miss—" the guard said. "Lady Liddy has been taken bad. She's having an attack, miss. I don't know exactly what—If you could come quickly—"

"Coming," said Cherry.

Martha Logan said, "I'm coming with you."

They went downstairs, the guard leading the way, explaining. Lady Liddy had come downstairs to ask Mr. Carewe a question, and to answer it, he had escorted her to the library. While consulting some books together, Lady Liddy had had a dizzy spell, grown faint, and collapsed, the guard said. "We all rushed to help her, miss, but we can't bring her around—"

He led them to the library. There the other guard, on his knees, was supporting the woman who was sitting, slumped forward, in a chair. Mr. Carewe was awkwardly holding a glass half filled with brandy, while the secretary rubbed the young woman's wrists. The librarian was pressing a dampened handkerchief to the back of the young woman's neck. Someone had removed her hat, exposing her frightened face.

"Eh, nurse?" Mr. Carewe said. "Will you see what you can do for her? We have telephoned a doctor, but he is many miles from here."

"I'll try, Mr. Carewe," said Cherry. She signaled Martha to sit down.

Then Cherry knelt, replacing the second guard. She held the young woman's thin wrist between her own thumb and forefinger. Her pulse count was normal—a little rapid, but normal. Her hands felt warm, which was normal. Cherry watched her breathing and counted her respiration rate—a little quickened, but not much and not shallow. Cherry placed her hand on Lady Liddy's forehead for a guess at her temperature. Her forehead was cool and dry—normal.

Cherry felt puzzled. If this were a fainting spell or a mild attack of some kind, where were the symptoms? The woman was trembling, but that could be from nervousness or fright, as much as from any faintness. "Careful," she thought, "I'm not a doctor. Perhaps I'm overlooking some symptoms."

"Lady Liddy," she said softly, "do you feel nauseated? Or are you in pain?"

The young woman shook her blond head, but murmured, "Headache."

Migraine? No, she showed no tension. Was she weak from hunger? Cherry asked, "Did you have an adequate breakfast this morning?" Lady Liddy nodded.

Miss Hayden asked, "Could it possibly be food poisoning?" But that would have produced a cold sweat and nausea, as well as faintness, Cherry explained. She bent and looked closely into the young woman's face and clear eyes. Lady Liddy self-consciously averted her head.

John Carewe said irritably, "Why don't you give her first aid?"

"I see nothing to give her first aid *for*, Mr. Carewe," Cherry said. She glanced at Martha Logan, who was looking as puzzled as Cherry felt.

"The best I can suggest, Mr. Carewe," Cherry said, "is that Lady Liddy see a doctor as soon as possible."

"Here, give her this." John Carewe thrust out the glass of brandy. "Revive her. Do her good."

The young woman refused the brandy. "I'm terribly sorry to be a nuisance." She sighed. "I often have these fainting spells. I'm—I'm simply not very strong, you see. It's nothing, really."

"Too much walking here this morning," Mrs. Ogilvie suggested soothingly.

"That's it," Lady Liddy murmured. "Thank you anyway, all of you kind people." She closed her eyes and took a deep, shuddering breath. Cherry wondered whether she was concealing some malady.

Martha Logan said, "Where is the Shah? Have we all forgotten to notify him that his wife is sick?"

"I'm afraid we did forget," said Miss Hayden. "Munro"—she addressed the guard who had summoned Cherry—"weren't you to bring the Shah when you went to bring the nurse?"

"I was unable to find the Shah, Miss Hayden," the guard apologized. "I did look around for him a bit, but in view of this lady's needing the nurse quickly—"

"You did the right thing, Munro," said Mr. Carewe. "Go fetch the Shah now, please."

The guard left the library. They all returned their attention to Lady Liddy, who swayed weakly in her chair. Cherry asked if there were some place where she could lie down, but Mr. Carewe said there was not—unless Lady Liddy wished to undertake traveling to his house.

"Oh, no, no," the young woman said almost in panic. "Thanks awfully, but I—No, really that's not necessary."

The old collector did not seem any too eager, either. Cherry glanced at Martha Logan. To Cherry's practiced eye, her patient appeared more drawn—and "keeping going on her will power"—than Lady Liddy. "I'd better pay first attention to Mrs. Logan," Cherry thought.

The Shah walked in, his mackintosh flapping and hanging bulkily around him, followed by Munro, the guard. When the Shah saw his wife, he gave a cry and ran to her as fast as his portliness would allow.

"My poor dear, not another attack?" He bent over her, his white beard brushing against her face. "My poor darling—I must take you to the doctor at once!"

"We've telephoned for the nearest doctor," Mr. Carewe said, "not very near, I am afraid—"

"No, no, we can't wait for the doctor to come here! Thank you, Mr. Carewe, you are most kind," the Shah said, and his voice rang out imperiously, "but I will take her to our friends' doctor, who knows her condition." He brushed aside reminders that the local physician was on his way. "Thank you, thank you, but no—My dear, can you stand if I support you?"

Cherry stepped forward to help, so did their host and both guards, but the Shah insisted he could manage unassisted. He did not even wish his chauffeur to be called.

"We've been through this ordeal before," the Shah said. "I have some medication in the car, to give Lady Liddy temporary relief. Now—up with you—very good!" He lifted the young woman to her feet. "Mr. Carewe, I am extremely sorry this depressing incident has happened in your house and that there is not time to discuss your magnificent collection—I owe you a thousand thanks—perhaps another time—"

With his arm around his wife, puffing from exertion and still talking, the Shah guided her from the library, through the foyer, and out the main door—quite rapidly. Miss Hayden had to hurry after them with Lady Liddy's handbag, which she had forgotten.

Their uniformed chauffeur, standing beside the imposing black car, sprang to open the car door for them and get Lady Liddy seated. He looked shocked—and something else. Cherry was struck by an unsuitable gleam in his expression, and then by the man himself. The chauffeur was stocky, powerfully built, dark-haired, and moved with vigor, as he jumped into the driver's seat. Not at all the well-trained chauffeur, who should have helped the Shah in, too. The chauffeur looked more like a man used to working with his hands, or perhaps he was the Shah's bodyguard. "Funny," Cherry thought, "I could swear I've seen this man somewhere before."

"You've forgotten your catalogues!" Mr. Carewe called, waving the two booklets.

"My dear Carewe, you must think me ungrateful," the Shah said, impatiently turning back for the catalogues. "I assure you I shall be profoundly in your debt—You have enriched us. Come and see us. My thanks to all—"

In haste the Shah trotted to his car, in such haste that he turned his ankle sharply. His left ankle, Cherry noted, as he caught his breath in pain. The Shah drew his coat around him and clumsily climbed into the car, slamming the door after him. Instantly the chauffeur started off, and the car streaked down the short driveway. The gate guard barely had time to open the entrance gate. The black car drove through and disappeared on the other side of the wall. They could tell from the motor's noise that the car was speeding along the road.

"Poor Lady Liddy must be dreadfully sick," said the librarian, "if they're obliged to rush her to a doctor at that speed." She shook her head in sympathy.

"Turned his ankle. Well," John Carewe said dryly, "now the doctor will have to have a look at both of them."

They all went back into the mansion. Cherry whispered to Martha that she would be wise to leave now, too. Martha whispered back that it was only eleven fifteen, they had forty-five more minutes left, and still a great deal to see. Mr. Carewe did not seem to expect them to leave, so she and Cherry started back upstairs. They climbed slowly, resting every few steps.

"Isn't the Shah fantastic?" Martha Logan said with a smile. "I'd hardly believe he's real, if I hadn't seen him on television."

"That beard!" Cherry said. "But what's on my mind is—what caused his wife to collapse. I couldn't say so, but I wonder if she was faking."

"Faking? Whatever for?"

"I can't imagine. Unless she was bored here and wanted to leave. Of course," Cherry said uncertainly, "I don't know how she *feels*—"

"Well—" Martha Logan started up the staircase again. "Out with the notebook. Back to work."

At a landing she paused. "Oh, look at these miniatures! We overlooked them before." She and Cherry studied the unbelievably detailed little portraits for several minutes, and made notes.

As they continued up to the second floor, the guard Munro came rushing down the stairs past them, crying out:

"Mr. Carewe! The Gainsborough in the Blue Room is gone—cut out of its frame! Mr. Carewe, sir! Four major paintings have been stolen from the second floor!"

Cherry and Martha stood aside as the white-faced guard ran past them. They stared at each other. Martha Logan said:

"This is terrible. I hope they don't suspect us. We'd better go right back to the library and tell Mr. Carewe we're willing to be searched."

"That bulky topcoat the Shah wore slung over his shoulders—" Cherry said. "He was alone on the second floor while we all were taking care of his wife—"

"Yes, I'm afraid the Shah had time to steal the paintings," Martha Logan said. "He must have carried a sharp knife and worked fast—"

"—and probably his topcoat has a false lining, so he was able to smuggle the paintings out of here," Cherry said. "Well, his wife *was* faking."

"At the speed their car was traveling," Martha Logan said, "they must be miles from here."

"What time is it?" Cherry glanced at her wristwatch. "Eleven thirty. Fifteen minutes since they left."

When they reached the office, Mr. Carewe was talking on the telephone to the police. He looked stunned;

his veined hand holding the telephone shook, though his voice was calm.

"—two Romneys, a Reynolds, and the Gainsborough. That connoisseur took our very finest paintings! Pardon?...Of course I am certain it was Shah Liddy! Hasn't all England been flooded with newspaper photographs of the Shah? Eh?..." John Carewe listened to the police at the other end. "No, I had not met the Shah before today....Very well, I shall not expect you to send out a nationwide alarm until you check....Yes. I understand....As I said, a rented car, a black Bentley. Its license number?...My guard at the gate and my other guests' driver believe its license number was—" He gave the number. "Yes, I shall ask the American ladies to stay here....Then I shall expect you very soon."

Mr. Carewe hung up. He did not repeat what the police had said to him. None of his subdued staff, much less his two American visitors, ventured to ask. The elderly collector buried his head in his hands for a moment. Then he recovered himself and gulped down the brandy he had poured for Lady Liddy. Cherry felt very sorry for the old man; they all did. They talked only a little, in low, shaken voices.

Within fifteen minutes, several detectives arrived. One detective, who said his name was Spencer, took Martha Logan and Cherry aside in the library, and quietly questioned them. He appreciated their willingness to be searched, he said, but it was unnecessary; obviously they were not the thieves. They answered all his questions—preliminary questions—to his satisfaction. They volunteered what information they could. The detective picked up Cherry's remark that she may have seen the Shah's chauffeur somewhere before.

"Would you think about that, Miss Ames?" the detective said. "We shall want to talk with both of you again today, after we've obtained more information. Will you stay here? Or where shall we find you?"

"At Wayside Inn near Windermere," Martha Logan said. "We're returning there as soon as you tell us we may leave...."

"Just a moment," Cherry interrupted. She saw with concern that Martha Logan all at once looked exhausted. The excitement of the theft and of being questioned by the police, on top of an hour and a half's close study of the collection, had been a great strain.

"Excuse me, Mrs. Logan," Cherry said earnestly, "but I don't think it's advisable for you to undertake the drive back to the Wayside Inn just yet. You'd better rest as soon as possible—no, not here. I know you don't want to impose on Mr. Carewe, as upset as he is. Anyway, I mean somewhere quiet where you can lie down."

"That's not a bad idea," Martha Logan admitted.

"Somewhere where you can have a quiet lunch, too." It was noon now. Cherry turned to the detective. "Mr. Spencer, is there any place nearby where we could go?"

The detective thought. "There is a modest inn about five minutes' drive from here. The Cat and Fiddle. Would that do?"

Cherry said that would be a great help. The detective offered to tell their taxi driver the route. He waited while they said brief thanks and goodbye to Mr. Carewe and his staff. The collector, between his distress and the presence of the police, scarcely heard them.

Then Mr. Spencer accompanied Martha Logan and Cherry out to their taxi. Edwin, their driver, was being questioned by a stout detective.

"All clear with this man," said the stout detective to Mr. Spencer.

"Very good, Geoff. I think the sergeant needs you in the house." Mr. Spencer turned to Edwin, and gave him directions for reaching The Cat and Fiddle. The driver soberly nodded and helped Martha, then Cherry, into the old sedan. The detective said to them:

"Wait for me at The Cat and Fiddle, will you please? I'll be along as soon as I can."

CHAPTER VII

At The Cat and Fiddle

AS THEIR TAXI PULLED OUT, THEY SLOWED AT THE GATE to let another car enter. Cherry heard the gate guard speak to the man driving. He was the doctor who had come to treat Lady Liddy. Cherry and Martha Logan exchanged wry smiles.

"Martha—just an idea—" Cherry said. "Would you like to have that doctor treat *you?*"

"So the poor man won't have come this distance for nothing?" Martha Logan joked. "Thanks, but all I need is what my nurse prescribed."

She leaned back against the seat and half closed her eyes. "How could a man of the Shah's eminence and wealth stoop to stealing? Trading on his famous name to gain entry to the museum—getting in past the guards—flattering Mr. Carewe into admitting him and his wife!" Martha shook her head. "I've heard about collectors with such a consuming desire to possess

102

fine paintings—or the money the art will bring—that they'll resort to underhanded methods. Bribery, trickery, shameless deals, a few even hire thieves. But what happened today—I can't believe it!"

"Martha, you mustn't allow yourself to become so excited," Cherry said. "Naturally, you're upset after the morning we've had. But please try to relax now."

Martha smiled and was quiet. Cherry called to their driver to go more slowly and gently. They drove along hedge-enclosed roads, with meadows and woods beyond. After a few turnings, they came to the inn.

The Cat and Fiddle was small and weather-beaten and must have been there a very long time, Cherry thought. They entered a modestly furnished sitting room, where a pleasant-looking man in a sweater came to receive them. He said he was Mr. Munn, owner of the inn, and he would be pleased, as they requested, to furnish them with lunch. He saw immediately that Mrs. Logan was tired. "If you wish to rest, madam, we have vacant rooms now that the season is over."

"Yes, thank you, Mrs. Logan had better lie down," Cherry said, over her patient's humorous protests. The innkeeper called, "Agnes!"

A tall, strapping, rosy woman wearing an apron came in. Mr. Munn instructed the maid to prepare a downstairs bedroom, and in a few minutes Cherry settled her patient there for a nap, closing the door. The innkeeper told Cherry that a hot lunch for them and their driver would be ready in about thirty or forty minutes.

"You might have a stroll in the garden, miss, or watch the telly," he suggested, and disappeared toward the back of the inn.

Cherry wandered into the sitting room. At the far end sat a plump little woman, half swallowed up in a huge wing chair beside the fireplace. The instant she saw Cherry, she started to chatter. Cherry sighed. She would have liked a few minutes to herself, to catch her breath and think about the morning's events. But the little woman—plump as a pigeon, dressed in an odd scramble of sweater, skirt, jacket, muddy walking shoes, handbag, ancient hat, eyeglasses perched on her freckled nose—was a determined talker.

"Bless my soul, a new guest! Quite rare here! I beg your pardon, but you and the other lady are Americans, I believe? I can always tell by your accent, though I fancy you can't help having an accent." She looked reprovingly at Cherry, who smothered a laugh. The woman went right on:

"You see, I myself am a permanent guest here, ever since my relations died. I'm the only one who resides here the year round. I daresay it's a sort of distinction."

"How do you do?" said Cherry, not knowing what else to say. Why, the poor old creature must be lonesome, marooned in this out-of-the-way inn year in and year out, with little to do or see. She was probably harmless for all her inquisitiveness.

"How do you do?" said the plump little woman. "I am Miss Pru Heekins. Most people call me Auntie Pru."

She reached out to shake hands vigorously with Cherry. Cherry shook hands and mumbled her own name.

"Welcome," said the little woman. "Are you a great walker? Your complexion inclines me to believe so. Unless—It's not rouge?" Cherry smilingly shook her head. "I myself am a great walker," Miss Pru Heekins rattled on. "I know every road, every house, even every car in this vicinity, and what's more, I am observant. Agnes, I am sure, believes I lead an idle, gossipy life, but Agnes is decidedly mistaken! Even when I am dozing a bit in this chair, or sitting outside napping in the sun, actually"—Auntie Pru leaned confidentially toward Cherry—"I am observing. Watching, listening, taking an interest."

Cherry thought eavesdropping was the word for Auntie Pru's curiosity. But she had seldom seen anyone so lonesome as this odd little leftover person. Cherry said, "Perhaps Agnes doesn't think any such thing about you. In any case, don't you worry about it."

"Thank you, my dear, you are very kind. I noticed you were very kind to the lady with the bad arm, too. Is she your aunt?" Auntie Pru demanded. "You don't appear the right ages to be mother and daughter, am I right?"

"Oh, you're absolutely right," Cherry said, gulping down another laugh. "I'm the lady's nurse, while she is making a—a business trip."

"O-o-oh, a nurse! No wonder you have some proper feeling for others," Auntie Pru said. "Not at all like that other young woman staying here. She's rather upstage, that young Mrs. Greene. Barely speaks to me, goes off for walks by herself, though you'd think she'd be glad to have company. Of course she did explain, when she arrived a few days ago, that she's convalescent and came to take the country air. But do you think," Auntie Pru asked aggrievedly, "that that is sufficient reason for not telling me even the simplest, smallest fact about herself? And we the only two guests here!"

"Perhaps she's just reserved," Cherry said, secretly admiring such resistance to Auntie Pru's onslaughts. Cherry thought how Auntie Pru would enjoy herself when news broke of the robbery at the nearby Carewe Museum.

"Would you turn on the television?" said Auntie Pru. "Time for the news soon, you know. I never miss it."

Cherry turned on the television set. Before the newscast came on, she went to have a look at her patient. Martha was asleep, so Cherry softly closed the door again and returned to the sitting room. Auntie Pru welcomed her back like an old friend.

They watched the newscast, which originated in London. After several items of major interest, a picture of the Shah and Lady Liddy flashed on the screen, alighting from a commercial airliner with other notables in a glare of flashbulbs. Cherry sat up with a start. The airport was Rome, and the broadcaster was saying:

"—Liddy arrived in Rome at midnight last night, after a visit to England. British reporters had not known of his departure from England, because of the suddenness of the Shah's decision to visit art exhibits in

Rome, which were scheduled to close soon. The Shah, interviewed in Rome, expressed his admiration for the art collections in London. Traveling on the same plane were Vice Admiral—"

Cherry did not listen to the rest. The Shah and his wife in Rome last midnight! So it was scarcely possible that they were here in the north of England at ten fifteen this morning. Then the Shah at the Carewe Museum this morning was an impostor—someone posing and acting a flamboyant role that, with a false white beard, was not too hard to fake—someone short and portly enough to resemble the Shah.

Short and portly, arrogant, left-handed—Cherry realized that the pretended Shah reminded her very faintly of someone. Who else that she knew was short and stout, bossy and conceited, and left-handed?

Why, Archibald Hazard was a great deal like that. But how absurd!

"Or *is* it so absurd?" Cherry asked herself. "Soon after Martha introduced Mr. Hazard to Pierre Selsam, the Selsam Gallery was burglarized. That might be a coincidence, of course. But isn't it quite a coincidence that the fake Shah and his fake wife turned up at the Carewe Museum *exactly when* Martha and I were there?"

That meant the impostor knew in advance that the Carewe Museum would be open for these visitors on this date—and at this hour. Certainly it would be easier for the thief simply to show up at the same date and hour—rather than risk applying in advance for admission—and walk in the front door in the guise of a distinguished visitor.

"Who knew that Martha and I were to he admitted at this date and hour?" Cherry asked herself. Their families knew, of course. She did not recall any news account about Martha Logan's trip that gave the exact date. Had she mentioned the date and hour to Peter, or to anyone else? Cherry thought back to her various conversations with Peter, then to the long conversation on the plane with Peter and Mr. Hazard. That was it! That was when Mr. Hazard had scraped an acquaintance with Martha Logan and egged her on to talking so much! Mr. Hazard had talked about the Carewe collection so knowledgeably, so amusingly that he had disarmed Martha—and led her into disclosing the date and hour of their appointment to view the Carewe collection.

So Mr. Hazard had made use of Martha. He had made use of her another time, now that Cherry thought about it! When he had entertained Martha and her at lunch in London, he had practically invited himself to go along with them to meet Pierre Selsam. The gallery owner had them on tour, and when they came within view of the rear door, she remembered, he had mentioned the night watchman on duty in the alley. Cherry wondered, appalled, whether Hazard could have had anything to do with the Selsam Gallery robbery. But, she thought, anyone of the hundreds of visitors to the gallery could observe its layout. Anyone could read up on which paintings were the most valuable. Anyone who wanted to could observe when and where the night watchman patrolled, and when the police patrolled the neighborhood. No, her suspicion connecting Mr. Hazard with the Selsam burglary was farfetched.

Someone poked Cherry. It was Auntie Pru, red in the face with excitement. "You aren't paying attention, my dear child! Listen—" She pointed to the television screen.

A regular broadcast had been interrupted so that an announcer could bring them a special bulletin—four paintings in the famous Carewe Museum had been stolen that morning.

"The Windermere police," the announcer went on, "report that a man posing as Shah Liddy gained admission with his wife. While his wife feigned an attack of illness, thus distracting the guards' attention, the man cut four priceless paintings from their frames and smuggled them out in a bulky topcoat he was wearing. The couple made their getaway in a rented black Bentley, driven by a chauffeur in regulation uniform—"

Auntie Pru clutched Cherry's arm. "A black Bentley, did he say! Why, I—" She babbled something unintelligible.

The announcer was saying, "Whoever the thief is, he is an art expert. The Gainsborough he took is the finest example of—"

Art expert, Cherry thought. Mr. Hazard is not really an art expert, but he knows some fundamental facts about art and art history—and the market value of great paintings. . . . Then it dawned on her that the dowdy little woman beside her was wildly excited.

"I saw a black Bentley on a road near here," she chattered, "while I was taking my usual long morning walk! Oh, dear, an American might not understand—the Bentley is one of those frightfully expensive cars, only a few rich persons can afford them. No one around here has one, or I would know it. You can be sure my eyes popped," said Auntie Pru, "when I saw a Bentley on our country roads! At nine thirty in the morning! And that's not all!"

Nine thirty that morning, on a road near here . . . The Shah and his wife had arrived at the Carewe mansion in a black Bentley at about ten fifteen. . . .

The special bulletin ended. Cherry turned off the television set, to pay full attention to her companion.

"My goodness," Auntie Pru said importantly, "I had better ring up the police! I have a duty to report having seen that particular car, haven't I?"

She marched over to a writing desk on which stood a pay telephone, her back erect, eyes glistening. Cherry could not spoil her fun by telling her the police were coming soon to The Cat and Fiddle, anyway.

"This is The Cat and Fiddle's only telephone," she advised Cherry. "Agnes has openly hinted that I listen to other guests' telephone conversations on this telephone. However, I told Agnes this is a public room. I can't help it if—Hello! Operator? . . . I want to speak to the police!"

Auntie Pru's triumphant glow faded as the police took her information and cut short Auntie's long-winded conversation. Then she listened, perked up again, and hung up with a flourish.

"Some detectives are coming here to consult *me,* if you please!" Auntie Pru bounced down into the wing chair. "And that's not all I can tell the police! I say, now that I think of it—Shall I tell you what else I saw?" She scarcely waited for Cherry's reply. "I saw Mrs. Greene, you know, that uppity blond young person who has been staying here—Well, I wasn't exactly following Meg Greene," said Auntie Pru, "it simply happened she was walking ahead of me on the road, a good bit ahead. And then, down the road comes this black Bentley. It stops for Meg Greene, and in she hops as smart as you please. Not a moment's hesitation—you'd think they had made an appointment. Then away they went and passed me on the road."

"Are you certain you saw this?" Cherry asked, a little stunned.

"Certainly I'm certain!" Auntie Pru Heekins snapped.

"You said Meg Greene is blond?" Cherry repeated. "Rather thin and frail looking? Medium height?"

"Why, dear me, yes! How did you know?"

"I—uh—I may have met her," Cherry said. "Did you see the chauffeur and the fake Shah in the car?" Cherry asked. "With a white beard."

"Didn't see either of them," Auntie Pru reported firmly. "I did see a heavyset man driving the Bentley.

He was wearing sunglasses and a hat. He sounded his horn when I didn't jump out of the car's way as fast as he would have liked."

The driver might have been Mr. Hazard, Cherry thought. Where had the uniformed chauffeur been? That question could wait, though—Auntie Pru was talking away at a great rate about Meg Greene.

"As I told you, this lah-de-dah Mrs. Meg Greene," said Auntie Pru with a sniff, "came to The Cat and Fiddle a few days ago, Wednesday last I believe it was. I happen to know she had made an advance reservation by telephone, from London, but that's incidental, isn't it? Said she needed country air and walks. In fact, immediately after she arrived, she took quite a long walk. Such airs as Mrs. Greene gave herself! Nobody was good enough to walk with her, though I offered in the *friendliest* way," said Auntie Pru. "No, she needs must always go alone. So I took my walks by myself. Once I came within sight of her unexpectedly—when I reached a crossroad, she was up ahead—and do you know what she was doing?"

"What?" said Cherry, picturing these lonely, empty country roads.

"There stood Meg Greene, in the middle of the road, sketching and scribbling something on a piece of paper. Now! What do you think of that?"

Cherry thought Meg Greene—*if* she were the same young woman who had posed as Lady Liddy—might have been sketching a route for the getaway car. But Cherry did not say so to Auntie Pru, for it was only a strong suspicion, not yet fact. Anyway, Auntie Pru's question was rhetorical; she rushed on:

"Another time after that—yes, I admit I was inquisitive enough to follow Meg Greene, you know, at a discreet distance," said Auntie Pru. "Well, she walked all the way to the village, and do you know what she did there? She mailed a letter. Pshaw, she could have left her letter on the tray in the lobby for Mr. Munn to post as we all do—"

Didn't Meg Greene want to leave her letter in full sight, Cherry wondered, where Auntie Pru or anyone else could read the name and address? Or did Meg Greene just want a reason and destination for a long walk?

"And that's not all!" Auntie Pru crowed, delighted by Cherry's interest in her story. She pointed a stubby finger. "I want you to notice particularly that telephone! And that writing desk!"

It was an ordinary telephone, and an old writing desk covered with a desk blotter. Beside the inn's one telephone, the desk held an old fountain pen in a stand. Auntie Pru confidentially advised Cherry that the pen was leaky, then remembered her main point—the telephone.

"I can tell you it was quite an event, my dear! Lucky for me I was in this room at the time," Auntie Pru said. "It's rarely enough anyone rings up here from the village or occasionally from Chester—hardly ever from London—and Meg Greene's husband telephoned her here from *Edinburgh!*"

Why Edinburgh? He could be there on a business trip, Cherry told herself. And was the man who had telephoned the same man who drove the Bentley?

Since forty-five minutes after getting into the car with him Meg Greene had posed as Lady Liddy, it seemed likely the short, portly man had assumed a white beard and the Shah's personality. Was that short man really Meg Greene's husband, or just a fellow thief? Cherry wondered why he had telephoned the blond girl, and—Cherry asked Auntie Pru—when.

"Let me see, it was Saturday evening. Day before yesterday. And I'll tell you something else interesting— Meg Greene took no walks last Saturday. I fancy she was waiting in for her husband's telephone call. Well! The telephone rang, and as I was sitting nearby, naturally I ran and answered it. Operator said 'A call for Mrs. Greene from Edinburgh!' I fetched her, then I sat down and didn't budge from this chair while she and her husband had a bit of visit. I was pretending to read, you see. Unfortunately," Auntie Pru said in disappointment, "I couldn't make out what *he* said, because what *she* said was awfully brief—rather tight-lipped, closemouthed, you know? If I had a husband, I would talk to him more nicely than that."

Cherry asked, "How do you know it was her husband?"

"Oh, she said as much to me and Mr. Munn and Agnes, after she hung up." That proved nothing, Cherry thought. "She wrote down something he told her, too," Auntie Pru recalled, and Cherry pricked up her ears.

"First, she listened quite a long time, and said 'Repeat that.' Then she said 'Righto. I'll remember that.' Then she listened again and said 'Repeat that slowly, will you, while I write it down.' So she took that leaky pen and wrote—"

"She did!" Cherry exclaimed. She sprang up to take a look at the desk blotter.

The blotter was fairly fresh, with here and there an ink blot, and snatches of reversed handwriting. By using her compact mirror, Cherry was able to make out a few words or parts of words, but they made no sense, and anyway, here the ink looked faded. The freshest, most recent-looking entry—and this was in a different hand from the other writing on the blotter—appeared to be an address. No, a telephone number—Muir 2361. Cherry wondered whether it was an Edinburgh number, since the call to Meg Greene had come from Edinburgh. Cherry copied the telephone number in a small shopping notebook in her purse. The attention of the police should be directed to this blotter.

"What are you doing?" Auntie Pru asked suspiciously.

"Just making a note of what Meg Greene wrote down."

Cherry checked the blotter minutely. She recalled Auntie Pru's report—Meg Greene saying "Righto. I'll remember that." Remember what? A street address? If not, it was something simple enough or brief enough to remember without writing it down—perhaps a name?

"Whatever do you want to do that for?" Auntie Pru persisted.

At that moment Martha Logan walked into the sitting room, looking refreshed. To her astonishment, Cherry gave her a vague "hello" from the writing desk, while bending over the desk and peering into the mirror of the open compact in her hand.

"What are you doing?" Martha asked.

Cherry turned around from the desk. "—uh—" She gulped apologetically. "Why don't you talk with Miss Pru Heekins, here, while I—*Please,* Mrs. Logan!"

"Oh. Certainly." Martha recognized Cherry's urgency. "May I sit with you, Miss Heekins? Have you been at The Cat and Fiddle long?"

Auntie Pru at once loosed a torrent of talk at this newcomer. Martha Logan, taken by surprise, defenseless, looked in Cherry's direction with an expression that asked, "Why did you do this to me?"

Cherry signaled back, "Sorry—something urgent—" No, the blotter held no other entry in the same handwriting, and Agnes must have emptied the wastebasket. Well, it was not up to her but to the police to search further.

Cherry rescued her patient from Auntie Pru, just as Mr. Munn came in to say that lunch was served.

"Sorry it took so long to prepare," Mr. Munn said, leading the way to the dining room. "Where is Mrs. Greene, I wonder? Hasn't she come in yet for lunch?"

Meg Greene was never coming back to The Cat and Fiddle, Cherry thought, but said nothing. She did not want to unleash another deluge of talk from Auntie Pru, who sat down at a table with a little bunch of flowers and a napkin ring—apparently her usual table. Mr. Munn seated Martha and Cherry at the far end of the room.

Agnes served them a good meal. Martha ate well, and Cherry was relieved to see how a little sleep and food revived her. Only toward the end of lunch did Cherry tell her Auntie Pru's story.

Martha at once saw the significance. "I'm fascinated," she said. "But how reliable are her 'facts'?"

"Auntie isn't the brightest person in the world," Cherry admitted. "Still it's possible she saw and heard pretty much what she insists she did. Allowing for certain inaccuracies—the police will know how to evaluate her story."

Several detectives arrived as the three guests came out of the dining room. Auntie Pru was all a-twitter to see them, coquettishly adjusted her ancient hat, removed her glasses, then put them on again because she bumped into Mr. Spencer. He seemed to know Auntie Pru, or at least to know who she was. So did the inspector and the stout detective. Martha Logan whispered to Cherry that some additional men had joined them.

The detectives put most of their questions to Auntie Pru. They seemed inclined to discount her reliability as a source of information at first, but Auntie Pru told the same consistent story she had told Cherry, then dramatically led them to the writing desk. The detectives were very much interested in the telltale blotter and removed it for laboratory examination. One man at once got to work on the phone to trace the call from Edinburgh.

The detectives made a systematic search of the room Meg Greene had occupied. She had left behind a cheap suitcase, a few inexpensive garments from which all labels had been carefully removed, and some toilet articles. The detectives impounded these for further study. They also examined the room for Meg Greene's fingerprints, and examined the contents of her wastebasket, which Agnes had emptied that morning. Apparently none of these things provided clues.

While this was going on, other detectives questioned Mr. Munn and Agnes. The innkeeper said, "Mrs. Greene told me she would leave sometime today, and she paid her bill this morning before starting out for her walk. I offered to drive her to the nearest bus stop or railroad station, since there is no taxi service here, but Mrs. Greene answered me in a vague way— evasively, I see now."

The quiet detective, Spencer, again talked with Cherry and Martha. "Your description of Lady Liddy tallies exactly with Mr. Munn's description of Meg Greene, no doubt about that," the detective said. "However, she's evidently an assistant in a carefully planned scheme. The man who posed as the Shah—he's probably the key man. He's the man we want. Can you tell us something further about him?"

Cherry hesitated. Had she any right to voice her suspicion that the impostor might be Archibald Hazard? But it was only the slimmest of suspicions, based on a commonplace physical resemblance and a knowledge of art. Neither trait was unique to Mr. Hazard. Cherry kept quiet. She remarked only that the pretended "Shah" was left-handed and had turned his *left* ankle in his haste at leaving. The detective already knew that.

Martha Logan could only repeat the same description of the thief. The detective said dryly that with the addition of disguising clothes and beard, he tallied with the description of the man whom Auntie Pru had seen driving the Bentley.

"He and Meg Greene must have changed into their disguises somewhere near here," the detective said, "between the time Auntie Pru saw them meet on the road and the time they arrived at the Carewe Museum. Their chauffeur must have joined them somewhere nearby, too. About that chauffeur, Miss Ames—if you are able to remember where or when you may have seen him before, will you notify us?"

Cherry said she would, and tried to think where she had seen that uniformed chauffeur before. It was hard to remember in the midst of today's excitement. Where else had she seen a dark man in chauffeur's uniform and cap? . . . Martha Logan gave the detective the name of the hotel where they would stay in Edinburgh, on the slight chance they might be needed. Mr. Spencer then said that they and their driver, Edwin, were free to leave.

Auntie Pru rushed over to say goodbye to Cherry, shaking her hand and holding up a magnifying glass that she had importantly produced.

"It's my embroidery magnifying glass," Auntie Pru said breathlessly. "Perhaps I can be of further aid to the authorities, seeing as I've been of outstanding aid already—the sergeant said so!"

"Well, congratulations—and goodbye, Auntie Pru," said Cherry, trying to pull her hand free.

"Goodbye, goodbye, Miss Nurse! I fancy you'll be reading about me in the newspapers. Oh, I say, if you ladies ever come by here again—"

They might never have escaped, except that another group of detectives came in and distracted Auntie's attention. One reported to the sergeant:

"I've found the rented black Bentley, sir. It was abandoned in a meadow out of sight behind a hedge, over near the woods. Three of our men are hunting through the woods."

The sergeant said, "Either those three are hiding in the woods—or more likely, since they shrewdly abandoned the Bentley, they are using other means of transportation to get away." He said this so calmly that Cherry realized the police, on a national alert, must already be watching all roads, buses, trains, and planes. The sergeant added, "A pity they had a little additional time to get away while we checked on the whereabouts of the true Shah Liddy. But, of course, as I told Mr. Carewe on the telephone, that had to be done."

Cherry would not let Martha stay to listen to any more. "We can hear about any developments on the radio or television," Cherry said. "Now you must go back to our hotel and really rest."

Edwin drove them quietly along the almost empty roads. Martha Logan murmured that this had been an extraordinary experience.

"I could mention something still more extraordinary," Cherry said. "Did it occur to you, as it did to me, that our friend in the beard and mackintosh may have been Mr. Hazard?" And she gave her reasons.

Martha Logan considered this, then shook her head. "You could be right, but I just can't believe it."

Cherry did not discuss the theft any further, in the interests of her patient's peace of mind and health.

For the balance of that afternoon they rested. That evening they packed. Next morning at nine they boarded another big tour bus for the all-day drive north to Edinburgh, Scotland. As the bus started off, Cherry was thinking: Muir 2361.

~~~~~~

CHAPTER VIII

Muir 2361

THERE WAS PETER! HE WAS HURRYING DOWN THE LOBBY as Cherry and Mrs. Logan entered the Edinburgh hotel. It was five o'clock. They had enjoyed the drive through steadily higher and wilder hills, crossing the border at Gretna Green for their first look at a Scottish village, then north, into this ancient, gray-stone city of battlements, castle, and churches. By now Martha looked very tired, and Cherry wished Peter could have bumped into them at a better moment.

"Hello, hello!" he said joyfully. "It's wonderful to see you both! How are you?" He shifted his armful of books in order to shake hands with them.

"How was the bicycle tour?" Martha Logan asked.

"Terrific! My students are enthusiastic. I'm just on my way to meet them to hear a lecture about Sir Walter Scott," Peter said. He exuded such good health and high spirits that Cherry beamed at him.

"How was your visit to the Carewe Museum?" he asked.

"A great treat," Martha said, "but we were there when that terrible robbery took place."

Peter frowned. "I heard about that—the press and radio are full of it."

"*We* didn't do it," Cherry said, to make him smile again. What was Peter looking so serious about?

"The darndest thing happened this morning—this noon," he started to say, then changed his mind. "Cherry, I must talk to you, but I see you and Mrs. Logan haven't even registered yet. Can you meet me here tomorrow, for lunch about twelve thirty?"

They agreed on that. Peter went off to the lecture. Cherry had Mrs. Logan sit down and ordered hot tea for her while she herself took care of registering. One of the hotel clerks gave Cherry their mail. It included letters from Cherry's family, letters from Martha Logan's children, and a telephone message from the Edinburgh police. It asked the two American ladies to telephone Inspector Forbes at a given number as soon as they arrived.

They were not surprised—they had told the Windermere police they were coming here. Cherry decided, though, to take care of her patient for a few minutes first.

Their high-ceilinged adjoining rooms each had featherbeds, which delighted Martha Logan. She lay down on hers, "just to test it out." Meanwhile, Cherry telephoned Dr. Malcolm MacKenzie, the orthopedist whom the London doctor had recommended. She succeeded in making an appointment for Martha Logan for the following morning at eleven.

Then Cherry telephoned Inspector Forbes. A matter-of-fact voice said, "We need to see you at our office immediately. Can you come?...Take a taxi. We will pay the fare."

"Just a moment." Cherry consulted Martha Logan, who agreed she was not feeling energetic enough to go and should ask to be excused. "Hello," Cherry said into the telephone, and explained. "Will it be all right, Mr. Forbes, if only I come?"

"Yes. Please be quick."

Cherry snatched up her handbag and coat and hurried downstairs and into a taxi. Driving across the somber stone city, she saw in the last light of dusk, high in the air, ancient Edinburgh Castle seeming to grow out of a great rock. How far she was from home, Cherry thought. She remembered uncanny Scottish ghost stories, tales of bloody clan battles and royal balls, and Tam o' Shanter's meeting with the witches at roaring River Doon. Here in the city, the streets already were half deserted, and dim street lamps flickered eerily in the cold, misty air.

The taxi let her out at a nondescript building. Cherry was ushered into a brightly lighted, efficient office that brought her back to the present with a jolt. Several detectives were at work at desks and telephones.

Inspector Forbes looked like a cross between a businessman and an Army officer. He had with him a handsome, well-dressed, dignified young woman. She was a policewoman, Sergeant Mary Jean Kerr, who would work with them, the inspector said.

"That is, I hope you are willing to work with us, Miss Ames," Mr. Forbes said. "I believe you were the first to discover the telephone number Muir 2361, of which the Windermere police notified us yesterday afternoon. Incidentally, their laboratory examination of the desk blotter from The Cat and Fiddle Inn didn't reveal anything more than you found....Yes, Muir 2361 is an Edinburgh number. I understand further, Miss Ames, that yesterday morning you were as close to the supposed Shah and his wife as I now am to you. Miss Ames, we need your help in identifying the suspects."

Cherry said, "I'd be glad to help in any way I can, Inspector Forbes." The young policewoman smiled at her.

The inspector nodded. "We have traced that telephone number to a shop that does fine needlework and—er—makes and sells doll clothes. A small shop, not prosperous, run by a Mrs. Kirby, a widow. She has no record that we can ascertain.

"We have observed the shop closely," Inspector Forbes said, "ever since the Windermere police notified us yesterday afternoon. So far we have seen only Mrs. Kirby, a few customers, and a needlewoman bringing in some work. Our men have, of course, followed these persons and checked up on them. We have also listened in, and checked on, all telephone calls to and from Muir 2361. Nothing suspicious, nothing revealing—so far," he finished.

Cherry thanked him for briefing her.

"Oh, yes, and we've seen a child of ten or twelve," the inspector added. "Neighbors say she is Mrs. Kirby's daughter, Amy. The child brings Mrs. Kirby lunch from a restaurant at eleven thirty, and eats with her mother in the shop. Then she goes back to school, our men report. Sometimes she runs out after lunch to bring her mother ice cream, or occasionally she returns to the shop after school. We have found no reason to suspect the child."

"If I may add something, sir?" Mary Jean Kerr said. "She's a quiet, nice little girl, very obedient—one would almost say, a far better child than one would expect an undesirable person like Mrs. Kirby to have."

"Quite true," Inspector Forbes said. "Now then, Miss Ames! Making a telephone call to Muir 2361 is where we need your help."

He pointed out that since Muir 2361 had originally been supplied to Meg Greene, alias Lady Liddy, whoever answered at Muir 2361 might expect to hear a feminine voice—might expect Meg Greene to call that number. Hers was an English voice. So Cherry's voice, with her American accent, would not do. The inspector said Sergeant Kerr would telephone.

"I'd like you to listen in," the inspector said to Cherry, "and tell me whether you can identify the voice of the person who answers."

It might be the shopwoman, or it might just possibly be Meg Greene or even the pretended Shah—though the inspector did not think that was likely.

"The shop probably is a front for the thieves, not a hideout," he explained to Cherry. "We have established that much by sending in a fire-department inspector to search the premises. Very likely the thieves know we are watching the shop, and so they won't use it for a hideout. Our men believe the thieves plan to keep undercover and use the shop as a relay station for messages. That's why the Muir 2361 number was passed along, probably. But *when* they will use it and *where* the thieves are hiding out—"

The inspector sat back, thinking. Then he signaled a man at another desk to plug in three extension earphones, one for the inspector, one for himself, and one for Cherry. Before the call to Muir 2361 went through, the policewoman asked Cherry to describe "Lady Liddy's voice—that is, Meg Greene's."

"Soft, hesitant, but then she was pretending to be sick," Cherry said. "That's not much help, is it?"

The inspector drummed his fingers on the desk. "It will be awkward if Meg Greene answers, but that's a chance we have to take. You had better say—or hint—that you are a friend of Meg Greene's," the inspector told Mary Jean Kerr. "And if Meg Greene does answer, improvise."

Sergeant Kerr nodded. The phone at the other end rang repeatedly. No one answered. They waited a few

minutes, then telephoned again. Still no answer. Inspector Forbes advised Miss Kerr she might as well hang up.

"It's well after six," he said. "The shop is closed. We
will try again tomorrow. Miss Ames, can you come back
here between nine thirty and ten tomorrow morning?"

"Yes, Inspector Forbes."

Cherry returned the next morning, and they put
through the call again. This time, at the other end of
the wire, a woman answered testily. Cherry, listening
in, signaled that this was not a voice she had ever heard
before. The detective who was listening in wrote on a
pad: "It's the shopkeeper—Mrs. Kirby."

"A friend of mine gave me your number," the young
policewoman said into the phone. Her voice held hints
and promises. "My friend said you might be more or
less expecting a call from her."

"Your friend? What friend?" said the voice, suddenly
roughened with suspicion.

The policewoman said smoothly, "Excuse me if
I have the wrong number. I had just better not try to
deliver her message—"

"Wait a moment!" the voice said. "What message?
Can you tell me your friend's name, miss?"

Sergeant Kerr hesitated. The inspector shook his
head—Meg Greene might be with them. The policewoman said into the phone, "I do dislike telling too
much on the telephone, don't you? I'd ever so much
rather come to see you." While they fenced verbally,
Inspector Forbes scribbled a note and pushed it toward

the policewoman: "Pretend you don't know where Muir 2361 is." Sergeant Kerr said into the phone, "You know, I have only your telephone number. I'll need your address, please—and what time shall I come?"

The shopwoman's voice floundered. "You're making a great nuisance for me, miss, especially as I—as I needs must see my dentist today. He—uh—hasn't said what hour. So if I can telephone you at two o'clock today? ... Not earlier, miss. Then perhaps we can arrange something."

The inspector muttered, "She wants time to get instructions." He advised his assistant to double the detail watching the doll-clothes shop.

"Two o'clock will be convenient," the policewoman said into the phone. "The number where you can reach me is—" She gave a special telephone number that, Cherry understood, would reach this police office but would not reveal that fact to the thieves. "Yes, I'll surely be here. Goodbye."

Inspector Forbes turned toward Cherry. "Miss Ames, I regret cutting into a visitor's limited time, but we shall need you here at two." A speculative glint came into his eyes. "In fact, we may need you well into the afternoon, if you don't mind a bit of action."

Cherry tried to hide her excitement as she promised to return. The inspector then brought her up to date on what the Windermere police had discovered:

Not far from the Carewe Museum, near where the black Bentley had been abandoned, the police had dug up in the woods a false white beard, clothing worn by the fake Shah and his supposed wife, and the chauffeur's uniform and cap. These had been half buried in earth and leaves. Evidently all three criminals had entered the woods before the robbery to change from their own clothes into disguises, then after the robbery they had changed back again. For their getaway they must have had a second car. Police had found fresh tire tracks in the woods.

"Then the getaway car must have been driven into the area by the third thief—the chauffeur," Cherry said. "The fake Shah must have arrived there, driving the Bentley. Wouldn't that explain why Miss Heekins had seen only him, and not the chauffeur, in the Bentley before the theft took place?"

"It does, indeed," the inspector said.

"Do you suppose all three of the thieves are here—right now—in Edinburgh?"

"That's a possibility we must work on," the inspector told her. "Our chief interest, of course, is in the man who posed as the Shah—the key man in this theft.... Well, Miss Ames, shall we see you at two, then?"

Cherry nodded. It was a good thing that her patient's appointment with the orthopedist was for this morning, not this afternoon.

By a little before eleven A.M., Cherry had called for Martha Logan at their hotel and accompanied her to the office of Dr. Malcolm MacKenzie. Today was the great day when the cast on Mrs. Logan's arm might be removed. She and Cherry were hopeful as they walked into the orthopedist's waiting room.

They both nearly fell over in surprise. There, about to leave, was Archibald Hazard, his left ankle swollen and bandaged. His left ankle! The fake Shah had turned his left ankle! Mr. Hazard was speaking to the nurse about his bill, and did not see them for a moment. Cherry struggled to recover her composure. She decided instantly to challenge him. If she could get any response from him—He turned around and saw them. She had a glimpse of the blinding shock on his face—and suddenly there flashed into her mind's eye the image of the last time she'd seen Hazard, unexpectedly, standing in the street in front of the London restaurant with a stocky, dark-haired workman. Why, that's who the "Shah's" chauffeur might have been— the same rough, powerfully built man! She had been confused by seeing him in a chauffeur's smart uniform and cap, and not in a workman's rough clothes.

"How nice to see you again, Mrs. Logan," Mr. Hazard said, seizing the initiative. There was a slight tremor in his voice. "What a surprise, Miss Ames. I hadn't known you were coming to Edinburgh."

"If you had known," Cherry thought, *"you might not have risked coming to Edinburgh yourself."* Still, Mr. Hazard seemed calm enough, unafraid of them. And why not? Cherry realized he had no way of knowing that she and Mrs. Logan had visited The Cat and Fiddle Inn, and learned about Meg Greene. He still might think they were fooled by the impersonations at the Carewe Museum. She must be very careful not to put him on the alert now.

Martha Logan looked baffled. "Hadn't you intended to go from London to Paris, Mr. Hazard?"

"Oh, I changed my plans," he said. "Some friends of mine here urged me to come visit them, and on a sudden decision I—ah—flew up from London."

"He's lying!" Cherry said to herself. She asked conversationally, "Have you been in Edinburgh long, Mr. Hazard?"

He seemed rattled by her question. "I've been here several days. Since—ah—last Wednesday," he added. He pointed to his bandaged left ankle, grimacing. "I had a stupid accident the day before yesterday. Turned my ankle as I was hopping on a bus, and the bus started off before I was quite aboard."

Martha Logan noncommittally murmured her sympathy. Cherry thought how cautious he was to account for the injured left ankle. He could guess they had seen the fake Shah turn his left ankle day before yesterday. At any rate, he was being very cagey and plausible with them, taking no chances.

"A wrenched ankle can be awfully painful," Cherry said. "What a shame to have it happen on a holiday. You should have had your ankle treated immediately, Mr. Hazard, instead of letting a whole day go by. It must have swelled yesterday." She was trying to draw him out. He was egotist enough to rise to the bait.

"Oh, and how it swelled!" he said. "Not right after I turned it—no swelling until yesterday, and I didn't limp until yesterday."

So that the police, on watch right after the robbery for a fleeing man who had wrenched his ankle, had no visible sign of an injured ankle to guide them. The ankle had swelled only yesterday; by that time Archibald Hazard could have made it to Edinburgh, taking cover in a great city.

He unwittingly confirmed this. "I did go to a doctor yesterday, one of these fine and famous Edinburgh physicians, but" Mr. Hazard complained, "he is a general practitioner. I'm not satisfied that he helped me. Not enough to suit me. So I've consulted an orthopedist this morning. So much better always to avail oneself of the best services."

Yes, nothing but the very best of everything would do for Archibald Hazard, Cherry thought.

Martha Logan said that she hoped he would join them for lunch or tea within the next few days. From her faintly guarded tone, and the briefest glint in her eye, Cherry realized Martha was now suspicious of Mr. Hazard, and her invitation was intended solely to unearth information.

Mr. Hazard started to protest that he had so little time here, but Martha went on blandly, "We want to hear about your trip. I must tell you about the magnificent Carewe collection. Isn't it shocking about the robbery there?"

His face changed color. "Disgraceful," he said. "A loss to the nation. And the robbery at the Selsam Gallery!...So nice to see you. Give me the name of your hotel—" Cherry tried desperately to think how she could detain him—keep him from slipping away. "I may or not have time to see you again. Pleasant journey. Goodbye."

Archibald Hazard limped out of the doctor's office, and was gone. Gone!

"Cherry, your suspicions about him were right," said Martha. "You'd better telephone the police."

"Yes, immediately, so they can pick him up."

Cherry obtained from the nurse permission to use a phone in another room, where she could talk privately. She called Inspector Forbes. She quickly reported in full all she knew and suspected about Archibald Hazard. She reported having seen Hazard in London with the workman who later, dressed as chauffeur, drove the fake Shah's car.

Inspector Forbes's voice on the phone sounded impressed, even excited. "Good, very good, Miss Ames," he said. He asked her a few questions, then said, "Come in at two, as we said. We may have more information on Hazard by then." He rang off.

"I just hope they catch him!" Martha Logan said, when Cherry told her about the telephone conversation. "Mr. Hazard is conspicuous enough, limping along on that swollen ankle."

"He's also smart enough to keep out of sight," Cherry said dryly.

"Isn't Archibald Hazard the cool one to be using his own name, after what's happened!" Martha said. "Wait—he said he's staying with friends here, didn't he? Of course, he may be lying about that, too."

"What I want to know is—" Cherry paused, frowning, "what is Mr. Hazard doing in Edinburgh, anyway? Why *here*?"

The nurse interrupted them to say that Dr. MacKenzie would see Mrs. Logan now.

After so much excitement, the interview with the orthopedist was placid. Dr. MacKenzie had a skill that Cherry at once respected. First, he had Mrs. Logan's arm X-rayed, then talked with her and Cherry. How did the arm feel? How did the right hand feel? How was Mrs. Logan's general health? He checked her over, remarking that her pulse was "a wee bit rapid."

Martha Logan grinned. "That's because I—Miss Ames and I—are having an exciting time in your city, Doctor."

The nurse called the doctor into his darkroom to see the developed X-ray film. Dr. MacKenzie took a thorough look, then came back and said, "The bone has healed satisfactorily. We can remove the cast."

Cherry was as glad as Martha, who joked, "I'll miss that dear old cast. After wearing it for four weeks, it has become an old friend."

To remove the cast, the doctor used an electric cast cutter with a little round saw on the end. It worked quickly and easily. Once her arm was free, Martha Logan was surprised to find it stiff and weak, and also painful. Dr. MacKenzie said that was to be expected.

"If you wish, we can support the arm in a sling for a while, to make you more comfortable," he said.

"Unless it would be better to use the arm. I notice my elbow joint is stiff," Martha Logan said.

Dr. MacKenzie nodded. "I would advise no sling, and gradual exercise"—he described a few simple ones—"until the muscles and joints get back to normal. It will be even more important, Nurse Ames, to encourage normal movements as often as possible, using the elbow and shoulder joints. I should think that will be sufficient exercise, since this was a simple fracture, and Mrs. Logan's earlier exercises squeezing the rubber ball have prevented loss of muscle tone. Just be careful not to overtire your patient. And take good care of her skin." Cherry knew that after cast removal, the skin would have accumulated waste products and be sensitive to the touch. She would bathe the arm gently and apply oil to soften the crusty old skin. "Also, Nurse Ames," said the doctor, "you'll need to massage the arm daily."

"Certainly, Dr. MacKenzie," said Cherry.

That was all. As they left the doctor's office, noon church bells were ringing. It was a fine day and Martha laughed about the weather report: "Sunny, showers." She wanted to buy them each a corsage, to celebrate getting rid of the cast. But Cherry reminded her, "We'd be late meeting Peter for lunch."

Peter was already waiting for them at a table in the immense dining room, within view of Edinburgh Castle. He jumped to his feet as Martha and Cherry joined him. Then he noticed Martha's right arm was free of the cast.

"Congratulations," he said, helping them get seated. "To both of you."

They chatted a little. Peter seemed preoccupied.

"I have something to tell you that troubles me," he said. "Maybe it will make more sense to you than it does to me. Do you remember Rodney Ryder?"

They paused to order lunch. Martha said, "The droll young man who amused us so much in Stratford? Yes, of course we remember him."

"Well, I saw Ryder here in Edinburgh yesterday morning," Peter said. "About noon. He was at the Shakespearean loan exhibit—it opened Sunday." This was Wednesday. "Big hall, big crowd. If there hadn't been so many people to push past, I might have gone to speak to Ryder—or maybe not."

"You sound surprised at seeing him," Martha said to Peter. "He *was* awfully interested in the Shakespearean paintings, back there in Stratford. Evidently he was interested enough to come here to see the exhibit again."

"I wonder," said Peter. "Ryder was awfully ignorant. You'd expect a scholar to make a trip to see the exhibit again—but would you expect it of that lightheaded young man? And there's another puzzle. When I saw him yesterday morning, he wasn't at all that Rodney Ryder we knew in Stratford. He was serious, quiet and—er—sort of purposeful."

Cherry remembered that this was the same description of Rodney Ryder's personality given by his innkeeper when she and Peter went to look for him. She reminded Peter of the incident.

"That's right," Peter said. "Which is the true Rodney Ryder? He certainly didn't look frivolous yesterday morning—he was wearing a conservative gray suit and hat. I'm baffled."

"Could it be that he put on an act for us?" Martha said. "I would guess Ryder used you. He made himself entertaining to get acquainted with you, Peter, so he could use you—meet the curator through you, I'd say."

"But why?" Peter said. "I can't believe Rodney Ryder's motive was simply enthusiasm for the Shakespearean paintings. And why did he suddenly leave Stratford without a word to any of us?—after we'd played tennis together constantly and I'd lent him a book! It's not only rude, it's baffling."

"Yes, why?" said Cherry. "Especially why did Ryder go to the Shakespeare curator, Mr. Lawrence, without Peter's knowledge or permission, and pass himself off as Peter's friend or student, and then pump the curator for information? That bothers me."

They looked blankly at one another, stumped.

"Anyway, there was Ryder," Peter went on, "looking at the Shakespearean paintings with another man. And guess who it was? Remember that Mr. Haggard, or Hazard, on the plane?"

Cherry and Martha nearly jumped out of their chairs. "Archibald Hazard? With Ryder? Are you sure?" Cherry demanded.

"Yes, I'm sure," Peter said. "He was limping—had something wrong with his ankle, sprained, I'd say—"

Cherry exclaimed, "There's our answer! Peter, we saw Mr. Hazard just this morning, and he was in a great hurry to get away from us. Don't you see?" she demanded of the other two. "Mr. Hazard and Ryder are here in Edinburgh intending to steal some of the Shakespearean paintings—I'll bet you anything!"

Peter looked incredulous. Martha caught her breath, but asked, "How can you be so sure?"

"Look," Cherry said. "Mr. Hazard used your contacts—directly at the Selsam Gallery, indirectly at the Carewe Museum. In both places paintings were stolen. Rodney Ryder used Peter's contact to learn which of the Shakespearean paintings are the oldest, rarest, most valuable—that is, which ones to steal. And now Ryder turns up at the Shakespearean exhibit *with Hazard*. Don't you see?"

Martha said faintly, "Yes, I see."

"Well, I don't," Peter declared.

"We happen to know," Cherry said, "that the fake Shah who stole the Carewe paintings was Mr. Hazard." Peter's mouth opened. Cherry stood up. "Please explain to him, Martha. I'm going to phone the police about Ryder's being in Edinburgh with Hazard."

"Wait," said Peter. "I have more to tell you."

Cherry sat down again. Peter said he had felt so curious about Ryder, and still so annoyed with him, that he had followed the two men, unobtrusively, when they left the exhibit hall.

"I shouldn't say I followed them, I just happened to be going in the same direction they were," Peter said.

"I'm positive they didn't notice me. I kept quite a distance behind them. Anyway, they were talking together too intently to notice me. I saw them go into a restaurant"—he gave its name—"on George Street."

Martha Logan smiled. "I've heard of that restaurant. It specializes in roast beef, and, as Cherry may remember, our friend Mr. Hazard is particularly fond of roast beef."

"Here's hoping the restaurant people learned something more about him than we did. Thanks, Peter," said Cherry. "Excuse me, while I telephone."

She reached Inspector Forbes at once. He was extremely interested in what Cherry reported. He said he had no information on Hazard yet. With Cherry's new information, the police would now try to locate Ryder, or both men together. The inspector said his men were already systematically checking Edinburgh's hotels and lodginghouses. As for the shopwoman, she was under twenty-four-hour surveillance and would be questioned later.

"We don't want to arrest her just yet, because that would tip off Hazard and make him still more wary and harder to catch. If we arrested and questioned the shopwoman now, it's doubtful that she'd tell us anything of value. We have a small hope that she might lead us to Hazard and now—this other chap—Ryder. *If* she is panicky enough, or stupid enough.... Well, Miss Ames, in view of what you have just reported," said the inspector, "we shall strengthen our guard on the Shakespearean paintings."

"As you remember, Inspector Forbes," Cherry reminded him respectfully, "the paintings stolen from the Selsam Gallery in London—probably by Mr. Hazard—were taken during the night."

"And you feel Hazard may attempt a night theft again? It occurred to me, too," the inspector said. "You can rest assured that we shall keep an all-night watch. One more question. Is your friend, Peter Holt, with you now?...Oh, excellent. Will you tell him, please, that I need to talk with him about this Ryder chap. If Mr. Holt could come to my office at once..."

Peter was crestfallen when Cherry told him and Martha about the inspector's request.

"Doggone it, just when I'd excused myself from my students so I could lunch with you!" Peter said. "Each time I find you, Cherry, we get separated."

"I'll try to see you later today," Cherry promised. "Let's try for five o'clock in the hotel lobby."

Peter reluctantly left. Martha and Cherry finished their lunch. They remembered that Cherry had a two o'clock appointment with the inspector, and a promise of sleuthing or at least excitement for later this afternoon.

"If you want to come along, or even just go sightseeing," Cherry said, "you'd better take a wee rest first."

Her patient said "Aye," to a nap. Cherry escorted her upstairs to their rooms, promising to telephone her soon. Then Cherry set out to keep her appointment. A misty rain was starting to fall. She did not see Peter as she entered police headquarters, only a man in kilts.

~~~~~~

CHAPTER IX

The Doll-Clothes Shop

THE SPECIAL TELEPHONE AT POLICE HEADQUARTERS rang exactly at two. Mary Jean Kerr answered. The shop-woman said, "Very well, miss. You may come and talk to me this afternoon—*provided* you tell me right now the name of your friend who gave you this number."

Inspector Forbes, listening in, muttered that her boss undoubtedly had instructed her to say this. He nodded at the policewoman, who said, "My friend's name is Meg Greene." They all held their breaths, but the shopwoman—the go-between—seemed to accept the name. The inspector signaled the policewoman to ask when to come. Cherry, also listening in, heard the raspy voice answer:

"My name is Mrs. Kirby, I keep a doll-clothes and needlework shop." The shopwoman gave an address a few streets behind Princes Street, the main thoroughfare. "Will you—will you be bringing someone with you?"

The young policewoman managed to sound convincing. "Why, no, Mrs. Kirby."

"Ah! Come right away. I shall be waiting for you." The shopwoman hung up.

Inspector Forbes commented that there were two possibilities. Either Meg Greene was not with the gang, or if she was, they were expecting a message from someone else. "They're trying to outthink us." He turned to Cherry. He explained that there might be someone in or near the shop whom Cherry could identify—possibly one of the three criminals.

"Miss Ames," the inspector asked, "could you 'happen in' there and pretend you are shopping while our Miss Kerr is there?"

"Yes, Mr. Forbes," Cherry said. She thought of Martha Logan's interest in detective stories. Through the tall window Cherry saw that the rain had changed into no more than a mist or fog. "May I bring Mrs. Logan shopping with me?" she asked.

"Yes, so much the better—if she can join you quickly," the inspector said. "I want you to give Sergeant Kerr a few minutes alone first with the shopkeeper. Let her leave ahead of you so you don't appear to be together."

"I understand," Cherry said. "And after Mrs. Logan and I leave the shop, what shall we do?"

"Whatever you wish. If we need you further, we will get in touch with you at your hotel," the inspector said. "Thank you, Miss Ames." He hesitated. "We are working on your report about Archibald Hazard, but we have nothing yet."

Cherry used a police telephone to call Martha. The inspector gave her a few instructions. He advised that they meet at a big woolens store a block away from the doll-clothes shop, then walk to the shop, so their "happening in" would appear casual and natural.

Cherry walked alone to the big store. She waited there, just inside the door. Martha Logan arrived by taxi a few minutes later. She asked Cherry in a low voice, "Do I look as excited as I feel?"

"Yes, you do," Cherry said with a grin. "Now, we simply are going shopping, with our eyes and ears wide open—" She dropped her voice to a whisper, to brief Mrs. Logan on the situation. "The inspector has men posted inconspicuously near the shop, but we've got to be careful, all the same."

"And discreet," Martha Logan said.

They left the big woolens store and strolled down the block. In the cool, moisture-laden air, everything looked gray and dim; the passers-by and the crowded buses flitted past like ghosts.

As they crossed the street toward the doll-clothes shop, Cherry saw two men, not together, waiting at a corner. One man was reading a newspaper. The other man was thoughtfully smoking a pipe and gazing into a bookstore window. She recognized both men as detectives she had seen at police headquarters. A little farther away a tall, thin, blind man, wearing a pulled-down hat and dark glasses, very slowly felt his way along with his cane, pausing, moving, pausing.

"Oh, look at these enchanting doll clothes!" Martha exclaimed, planting herself in front of the shopwindow.

Cherry forced a smile as she came to look. Inside the rather bare shop she could see Mary Jean Kerr talking with a frowzy woman wearing a sewing apron. They seemed to be arguing. The woman angrily, repeatedly shook her head. Behind her, Cherry heard the faint tap-tap of the blind man's cane.

"Let's go in," Cherry muttered to Martha.

The shopwoman paid no attention as the two new customers entered. "Indeed I am not acquainted with any Meg Greene!" she was insisting to the young policewoman. "I'll thank you to stop talking in riddles, and tell me in a decent way who gave you my tele- phone number."

"But I have told you, Mrs. Kirby," said Mary Jean Kerr, with a show of anxiety. In her hat, coat, and gloves, carrying a parcel, she looked like any young housewife. "Meg Greene gave me your number."

"When?" the slovenly woman demanded. "And where was this Meg Greene?"

The policewoman answered, "She gave me your number day before yesterday"—that was the day of the Carewe art theft, Cherry remembered—"and she was telephoning me from the north of England. Ah, Mrs. Kirby! I don't dare say more than that! Please believe me."

The shopwoman fidgeted with her apron. "There's been a mix-up somehow, that's all I can believe, miss. I tell you, I've never heard of your friend, never."

The policewoman said pleadingly, "You may not know her, as you say, but she knows you—or knows *of* you. Will you just listen to the message?"

The shopwoman peered at her. "A message for who? Not for me, surely." The policewoman kept quiet. "Well? Well? Who's the message for?"

Cherry and Martha Logan pretended to be busy examining some doll sweaters on the counter. Out of the corner of her eye, Cherry noticed the blind man slowly passing before the shop.

"The message," said the policewoman, "is to call the number I gave you, at any hour of the day or night."

The shopwoman gave a contemptuous snort. "You may forget about such a message, miss. If there is trouble a-brewing, I want no part in it! Now excuse me, I must attend to these two ladies."

The woman bustled over to them. At Martha's request, she pulled out a box of doll dresses. She was still grumpy, not very obliging. Cherry noticed the selection was meager. The woman must have a hard time earning a living here—unless she kept the shop merely as a front. Martha Logan admired the fine handwork and bought several items.

Meanwhile, the policewoman had left. Her visit had yielded no information at all, Cherry realized. As soon as the shopwoman had wrapped their purchases, Cherry and Martha left, too. It was raining lightly again.

Coming out of the shop, Cherry all but bumped into the blind man. He was standing uncertainly on the sidewalk, as if waiting for someone.

"Oh, I'm sorry!" Cherry said. He grunted and gropingly moved a few steps away, so tall and thin he seemed to be on stilts. Didn't he remind her of someone? She could not see his face very well under his pulled-down hat. She had an impression chiefly of dark glasses and a mustache.

"Where will we find a taxi?" Martha was saying. Cherry did not answer. She had an uneasy feeling that the blind man was watching them. How fantastic! A blind man couldn't watch them. Yet the back of her neck prickled in terror—at sensing a hostile pair of eyes in back of her. Cherry stiffened.

"Let's walk to the corner," Martha suggested. She took Cherry's arm, and felt her tenseness. "Why, what's the matter?"

"I don't know," Cherry whispered. "Keep walking."

They walked away from where the blind man stood. Cherry forced herself to wait while a minute or two went by. Then she took one long look over her shoulder.

The blind man had taken off his dark glasses and was wiping the rain off them. But that's what a sighted person would do! Cherry tried to see his eyes—in the misty light and under his hat, it was hard to be sure—but she thought his eyes appeared normal. Yes, they *were* normal; as a nurse she recognized that much! How rapidly he was blinking, though—

Suddenly Cherry recognized him. Rodney Ryder blinked like that—and was grotesquely tall and thin. He hadn't worn a mustache the last time she had seen him, but she remembered his face. The mustache could be a false one.

He saw her. Cherry turned her head away but not fast enough—he had noticed her watching him! Like a shot he strode off in the opposite direction, in long, determined strides, putting on the dark glasses as he went.

Cherry started toward the near corner, to tell the two detectives of her discovery. They were already coming rapidly up the long block, watching the blind man. The detective approaching nearest to Cherry acknowledged her only with a sharp glance.

"That blind man"—she called out—"he's not blind!"

"Yes, we saw that, miss," the detective called back. "Look! He's getting away—"

"He's Rodney Ryder!" Cherry shouted. Turning again, she saw Ryder running, already halfway up the next block. Cherry broke into a run and went after Ryder. So did the detectives, still nearly half a block behind her. Martha, waiting bewildered in the rain, was left behind. As Cherry ran past the shop, she had a blurred impression of the shopwoman alone at the window, her face drawn with fear.

Cherry looked up the street where Ryder—now a distant figure nearly two blocks away—was reaching a cross street crowded with traffic. Cherry redoubled her speed. In back of her she heard one detective's pounding footsteps. Apparently the other detective was going to arrest or question the shopwoman. Up ahead Ryder swung aboard the open platform of a bus passing on the cross street. The double-decker bus stopped for a traffic light, and stood there.

Cherry ran that last block for all she was worth. Thank goodness the traffic light stayed red for a long time! She made it to the cross street, and without thinking, hopped on the same bus just as it started to move.

She stood on the open platform, panting, and looked back for the detective. Maybe she shouldn't be on this bus with Ryder. She could still jump off—It might be wiser to follow Ryder in a taxi—more discreet—but she couldn't see any empty taxis. The main thing was not to lose track of Ryder. The detective came running to the corner and Cherry waved to him. He saw her and nodded, and ran uselessly after the moving bus. Then he gave up and looked around for a taxi.

"Whew! I'm glad the detective saw me," Cherry thought. "I don't much like following Ryder on my own. I wonder if Ryder noticed me get on this bus."

Such a crowd was packed into the big bus, sitting and standing, that there was a chance Ryder had not seen her get on, and did not see her now. Cherry could not locate him inside the lower deck of the bus. Cautiously she climbed halfway up to the top deck, and saw Ryder's head and shoulders rising above those of the other passengers. Cherry came back down to the bus platform. The conductor asked for her fare.

"Yes—just a moment—" Cherry paid, then looked back for the detective. She spotted him in a taxi following the bus. Good!

For the next ten or fifteen minutes Cherry stood inside on the lower deck, half hidden in the crowd. The bus drove into residential streets. Cherry kept watching the bus stairs for Ryder to come down and get off. Occasionally she glanced toward the traffic, looking for the detective's taxi—yes, it was still following the bus. She'd better watch those stairs! Once the bus got snarled in a traffic jam. It started to move again, and after that the crowd began to thin. Tensely she watched the stairs....

Then she saw Ryder. He bolted down the steps, his hat pulled low over his face, and jumped off the bus before it came to a full stop. Cherry squirmed past the other passengers as fast as she could, calling to the conductor, "Out, please! Out!"

CHAPTER X

End of a Bad Actor

BY THE TIME CHERRY GOT ONTO THE STREET, RYDER WAS well ahead of her. Had he seen her? He didn't look back, if that was any encouragement. Was he leading her on a false trail?..."We'll soon find out," Cherry thought.

Ryder turned down a shabby, cheerless street. Rows of brick houses, all alike, reared up from empty sidewalks. In some of the windows were signs reading: BED AND BREAKFAST. Cherry rapidly turned down the same street, glancing at a corner street sign: *Weir Street.*

Ryder was hurrying, a dim, solitary figure in the rain. Cherry followed half a block behind, and saw him enter a house. She counted the houses and figured that the street number of the one he had entered was 26. When she reached the house, she saw that the window blinds were drawn. No one else was in sight. Cherry's wristwatch read four o'clock, too early for people to be coming home from work, too wet for strollers. She stared at the door.

"Do I dare go in? I didn't see Ryder use a key, so I guess the door's unlocked. Unless he locked it after him from inside."

Her first impulse was to go in immediately. But she paused to think. She looked back for the detective. No sign of him or a taxi. It would be foolhardy, even danger- ous.... Maybe Hazard was there too. She hoped so.... But then it would be even more dangerous.

"Yet I must not lose them," she argued with herself. "Maybe there's a telephone in the entrance hall. If no one's around I could slip in, call the police, and slip out again quickly. Then I'll watch for the detective in the taxi. He should be here any second.... I've got to take the chance," she decided.

Cherry knocked on the door, ready to run if she had to. No one answered. Her hands trembled as she tried the door. It opened, and she peered cautiously into the dark hallway. Leaving the door open, she stepped inside, blinking in the sudden dark.

The door swung closed. Cherry turned in confusion. A hand, hard and heavy, clamped over her mouth. She was jerked backward and held in an iron grip. Ryder, unseen, said quietly into her ear, "If you make a sound, I'll strangle you. I'll not have the neighbors hear you."

Next a handkerchief or a scarf was pulled tight across her mouth, so that she could only whimper. Where were the people who lived in the house? Where was the detective?

Her eyes, growing accustomed to the dark, saw Ryder's free hand reach out and bolt the door. He forced her to the staircase and started dragging her up. Cherry pulled back and kicked against the staircase railing to make noise.

"That'll do you no good, my girl," said Ryder. "There's no one here except a friend of mine, on the top floor. The respectable couple who rented us their spare room, as a favor to their friend Mrs. Kirby, haven't any other tenants. Just us two 'deserving schoolmasters.'" Ryder snickered. "And they themselves don't come home from work until well after six. So up the stairs with you, now! You thought in Stratford I was a silly fool, didn't you?"

Cherry glared at Ryder. He laughed in her face, and pulled her along up the stairs.

The stairs were narrow and steep. Cherry counted as they climbed: three flights to the top landing. Ryder still held her arm tightly as he knocked on the one door up here.

"I say, Archie! Open up! I've brought a guest," Ryder said.

Archibald Hazard unlocked and opened the door. He was in shirtsleeves and slippers. A sour smile spread over his face as he saw Cherry, and heard Ryder's brief account of how she had rashly followed him.

"I made quite a haul, what?" young Ryder said. "Two detectives spotted me."

"Detectives?" Hazard said. "Then get in here quickly."

"Oh, no one's coming," Ryder said offhandedly. "We shed one man near the shop. The other chap, in a taxi, got caught in traffic about ten or fifteen minutes ago. Meanwhile, my bus moved on."

Cherry's eyes flew wide open. She had not seen the detective get stuck in traffic. "I was too intent on watching for Ryder to notice," Cherry thought. "So the detective isn't coming—he can't, he doesn't even know where I got off the bus! I'm here alone in this house with Hazard and Ryder—and no one knows where I am!"

"For once you used your brain," Hazard said to Ryder, "when you let the girl in the house. Bring her in and we'll tie her up," Hazard ordered. He did not bother to speak to Cherry. "Now if we could get the Logan woman out of our way, too—"

Cherry balked, but Ryder shoved her into the room. She saw it was hopeless to resist—better to save her strength, in case she could find some way to escape later. Hazard locked the door.

The room smelled of stale coffee. It held a bed, a cot, two wooden kitchen chairs, an old bureau, and a shabby table with food, paper bags, and a revolver on it. Cherry looked around for a way out, but the only other door, standing open, led into a clothes closet. And the high dormer windows, recessed under the roof, would hardly be seen from the street. She was trapped.

Ryder pushed her onto a chair, finally letting go of her arm. Cherry rubbed her bruised arm. Then in one quick movement she tugged at the gag. Hazard slapped her hard across the face. For a moment she felt dizzy and blinded. When her vision cleared, she saw Hazard was holding the revolver.

"If you insist on being a nuisance, Miss Ames," he said in his usual courteous, pompous way, "you will force me to take drastic action. May I suggest that, if you wish to go on living, you stop acting like a fool. You've already been too smart for your own good, haven't you? Rod, haven't you found that rope yet?"

"Righto, here it is." Ryder came out of the closet, carrying a length of rope and a knife.

"Tie her hands behind her back," Hazard ordered. "Next, tie her ankles. Then tie her to the chair. Sit still, Miss Ames—or must I slap you again? Get on with it, Rod."

Cherry felt hot tears sliding down her cheeks. She was nearly as angry at her folly and helplessness as she was terrified. What did Hazard intend to do with her? At least he put the gun back on the table....She cringed with fear as the ropes bit into her. With her eyes she followed Hazard, limping around the room, and silently implored him to let her go.

Hazard addressed her with sarcastic formality. "I hope you will enjoy your stay here, Miss Ames. We have a job to do, and immediately afterward we're getting out of Scotland. You will remain in this room, tied and gagged, as our guest. I've already asked our landlords, the Martins, not to come upstairs here until Saturday, when Mrs. Martin can clean. Our rent is paid in advance to Saturday, so they have no reason to come up here. I doubt that the Martins will be able to hear any noise you might be able to make, since they occupy the ground-floor rooms."

Mr. Hazard made her a little bow, limped away, and sat down on the bed. Ryder sat beside him, changing his wet shoes for a dry pair.

"Any phone call from Mrs. Kirby's kid, Amy?" Ryder asked. "I mean to say, after I left off playing blind man?"

"No, the kid hasn't phoned here since lunchtime," Hazard said, "asking what to do about Meg Greene's 'friend' who telephoned the shop. That was the last phone call. I—um—don't expect to hear from Mrs. Kirby. Not soon, at least. Either she's lying low, or the police have arrested her."

Ryder looked up nervously. "Will she talk to the police?" Cherry's hopes rose, then died again as Hazard said:

"I doubt that she'll talk. I paid her well enough to buy her silence, if the police question her. And she needn't talk in order to save her own skin—she's in no danger, nothing wrong happened at her shop, actually."

"Well, will her kid talk?" Ryder asked, and answered himself. "No, the poor thing is scared to death of her mother. Even *if* the police would suspect a ten-year-old—"

In the midst of her own terror, Cherry pitied the child who had a criminal for a mother.

"Never mind the Kirbys," Hazard said impatiently. "The main point is that the police are suspicious about you and me, now. I've decided we'd better take the Shakespearean paintings tonight, and clear out of here."

"But can you do it with your bad ankle?" Ryder asked.

"There's no longer much choice. I'll manage. You're a great worrier, Rod," Hazard remarked.

Cherry listened numbly, as if she were having a bad dream. Ryder got up and paced around the room, passing Cherry as if she were a piece of furniture. Then he folded his long, thin body into the other wooden chair.

"I *am* worried about my wife," Ryder said. "I wish I could be sure that she's safely hidden at her mother's house. No phone there, or I'd call from Edinburgh as I did before."

"Shut up," said Hazard. "You're talking too much in front of the girl." He jerked his head toward Cherry.

"Oh, all right, all right," Ryder said resentfully. He sat brooding. Hazard stretched out on the bed. Cherry's attention wandered.

She was in such physical discomfort that she almost cried. Her lips under the gag felt dry and stiff. The harsh ropes confined her to one rigid, aching posture. She tried to think. The detectives must have reported the incident of the blind man to police headquarters. But they had no leads to 26 Weir Street.

Cherry turned her head and saw an alarm clock. It read ten to five. She was to have met Peter at five, at the hotel. Perhaps Martha would keep the appointment for her, to tell Peter that she, Cherry, was missing. If only Peter's talk with Inspector Forbes had uncovered some new lead, some way to find Ryder and this address! But the only information Peter had was the restaurant that Ryder and Hazard had entered yesterday, and that she had reported to Inspector Forbes by telephone at lunchtime.

"Surely the police have investigated at the restaurant by now," Cherry thought. "I guess they didn't learn anything, or they'd be here." She lapsed into a dull, blank despair. She could only sit immobilized and wish for a drink of water.

"Rod," said Hazard, sitting up on the bed, "lay out the things we'll need tonight. On the cot."

"Right." Ryder stood up and stretched, looking fantastically tall. Then he brought, from the closet to the cot, a small claw bar, a jimmy, a chisel, two flashlights, two small, sharp knives, all small enough to fit in a man's pockets, and a roughly sketched floor plan marked with X's. Cherry watched, half sick with helpless rage.

Hazard ordered Ryder, "Next I want you to pack our clothes. Pack tight—"

"I didn't hire on as your valet, Archie!"

"Just shut up and do as I say. Be sure to pack tight. Leave room for the rolled-up paintings." Hazard glanced sharply at Cherry, then ignored her again. "Let's eat early tonight."

The two men discussed getting food in for supper. Cherry gathered that Ryder had been bringing food in from a local sandwich shop, particularly since Hazard had been spotted by the American women at the doctor's office. It was clear that Hazard was not going to offer any food to their involuntary guest. . . . There was a sharp rap on the door.

Hazard and Ryder stiffened. They exchanged glances, but remained motionless and silent. Cherry thought of scraping or stamping her bound feet on the floor, to let the caller know someone was inside. But Hazard reached for the gun, and pointed it at her.

The knocking increased. A man shouted:

"Open up! Police! We know you're in there—we heard you talking. Open the door, or we'll break in!"

Hazard placed himself slightly behind Cherry in the chair. She realized what he was doing. If a gunfight broke out, she would be in the line of cross fire—and Hazard would use her as a shield.

"Open up!" the police shouted again. "We've got the stairs and all exits covered—this building is surrounded. The two of you haven't a chance!"

Ryder was tiptoeing toward the closet, but then—as the police rained blows on the flimsy door—Ryder seemed to change his mind. He ran across the room to Hazard. Hazard looked up at Ryder inquiringly, expecting the younger man to speak. Instead, Ryder struck him, threw him off balance, and snatched the gun out of Hazard's hand.

"All right, I'll let you in!" Ryder shouted. "I'm not such a fool as to shoot it out!"

Hazard lunged for Ryder, but Ryder knocked him down. Then Ryder sprang to the door, unlocked it, and flung it wide open. Six detectives stood at either side of the door, guns drawn. One was the detective who had tried to follow Cherry and Ryder.

As the detectives rushed in, Ryder cried out half-hysterically:

"You can't hold me on any charge! I was tricked into this! Hazard's the man you want!"

"You sniveling liar," Hazard sneered contemptuously. He picked himself up from the floor.

"Be quiet, both of you!" the detective in charge ordered. "Bally, Jock, untie the girl. Did they harm you, miss?"

She mutely shook her head. Two detectives freed her from the ropes, and looked at her carefully to see if she were all right.

Archibald Hazard limped over to the bed and sat down. He looked defiant. The chief detective, Graham Kerr—who said he was a cousin of the young police-woman, Mary Jean Kerr—told Ryder to sit on the bed beside Hazard. Then Sergeant Kerr came over to Cherry and asked solicitously:

"Sure you're not hurt? Can we get you anything?"

"A glass of water," Cherry said. "My—my hands and feet are numb."

Sergeant Kerr sent one man for a glass of water for her. Bally and Jock helped her to her feet, and rubbed her tingling hands.

"Sergeant," said one of the detectives, "have a look at what's on the cot over by the window,"

Kerr picked up the diagram with the X's. "What is this?" he asked. "Answer me, Hazard."

Hazard did not deign to answer. Ryder, trembling uncontrollably, shouted:

"I'll tell you everything you need to know! I'm sick of Archie Hazard's highhanded treatment and low pay! I'll tell you what it is. It's a layout of the exhibit of Shakespearean paintings—the X's mark the ones we planned to take....Yes! Yes!...We were going to do it tonight! Only let me off lightly—"

"Tell them," said Hazard, "about your wife. Or shall I?"

Ryder's mouth closed tight. He turned on the bed and lunged at Hazard. Sergeant Kerr stopped him with his fists and gave both men a sharp warning.

"You can talk at police headquarters. We're going there now. Will you be able to walk, Miss Ames? Our man will assist you down the stairs."

"Thank you," she said. "I'm feeling better."

She had to go slowly down the stairs. She leaned on the arm of Detective Cox, who had tried to give chase. "I had a bit of foul luck in that traffic tie-up," he said to her in apology. "You did a good job today, Miss Ames."

"I don't think I'd do it over again," said Cherry.

They reached the street. The rain had stopped. In the dusk a small crowd had gathered around the police cars. Detectives kept the onlookers back as Hazard and Ryder, handcuffed, were put into one car. Cherry rode with Sergeant Kerr, Cox, Bally, and Jock in another car. Kerr told Cherry that another detail remained in the house to collect the thieves' tools, search their room, and talk with the Martins when the landlords came home.

The police cars traveled much faster than the bus in which Cherry had reached Weir Street. She asked Sergeant Kerr, "How did you find out about 26 Weir Street?"

"We went to the restaurant on George Street," Sergeant Kerr said, "about one fifteen. We were unable to get any clue immediately, because yesterday's lunch waiters do not come in today until dinner hour. However, the manager remembered that a waiter called John waited on two men answering to Hazard's and Ryder's descriptions. The manager gave us John's home address and we looked him up.

"Unfortunately for us—and for you, Miss Ames—John was not at home. His wife said he had gone to the country for a hike, she didn't know exactly where—but would be home at four o'clock."

At four o'clock, Cherry recalled, she had been entering 26 Weir Street. The detective went on, "So we had to wait around until four, and then John came in. He remembered hearing Hazard say something about 'he didn't think much of Weir Street as a place to stay.' We came right over to Weir Street, of course on the inspector's orders. Then it took us a while to investigate several houses until we heard men's voices and conversation, which we—well, we thought sounded like what we were looking for."

"I had a narrow escape," Cherry murmured, and Sergeant Kerr said, "You did, indeed, miss."

The police cars drew up in front of headquarters. Hazard and Ryder were taken inside. As the detectives helped Cherry out of the car, she saw Martha and Peter getting out of a taxi. They hurried over to Cherry, relief and concern mixed in their faces.

"Thank heavens!" Martha exclaimed. "Cherry, you look shaken. Are you all right? What happened?"

Cherry told them briefly, as they went into the building and waited, as requested to do, in an anteroom. Peter was speechless. Martha looked rather sick.

"We've all been worried to death about you," Martha said to Cherry. "After you and that detective went running off, Mr. Blair—he's the other detective who was posted near the shop—notified Inspector Forbes by telephone. Then we came here to report details. The inspector was reassuring me that Mr. Cox would look out for you when"—Martha shook her head—"Mr. Cox walked in *without* you. Said he'd lost you! Well!

"But a minute or two later, the inspector had a phone call from Sergeant Kerr, who'd just learned from the waiter about *somewhere* in Weir Street. That gave me a little hope," Martha said.

"Poor you," said Cherry.

Martha shrugged. "Inspector Forbes finally persuaded me to go to the hotel and rest. But how could I rest? I waited until Peter came in at five, and told him you were missing, and—Well, we came here hoping we could help."

"If I'd known earlier—" Peter said. "I feel awful about what you've been up against, Cherry."

Cherry looked down at her sore, rubbed wrists. "I've been an idiot."

"But such a nice, well-meaning idiot," said Martha. They all had to laugh.

Sergeant Kerr came out of the inspector's office and asked the three of them to come with him. They entered a glaringly lighted office with barred windows. Armed guards stood at the room's two doors. A policeman stenotypist came in. Then Hazard and Ryder were brought in by the detectives who had captured them. When the inspector came in, everyone sat down. Cherry noticed Hazard's and Ryder's inky fingertips; the prisoners had been fingerprinted.

The inspector said, "We are going to take down preliminary statements from Archibald Hazard and Rodney Ryder. They will have benefit of counsel and a trial in due course. I should like our American visitors to listen, in order to verify or challenge anything in the statements of which they have firsthand knowledge. Mr. Hazard, we will begin with you."

Sergeant Kerr prodded Hazard, who sullenly stood up. "By the way," the inspector said, "we've been checking this afternoon by radio with the police in New York City, with Scotland Yard in London, and with Interpol headquarters in Paris, on the four criminals in this case. So you may as well talk, Mr. Hazard."

Hazard stubbornly refused to say a word.

"Very well, Mr. Hazard," the inspector said. "I shall read you Interpol's dossier on you." He picked up a typed report. "'Archibald Hazard, forty, American. Real name Fred Walker. Several aliases given. Early in his life was an unsuccessful actor; now uses his skills in acting and makeup to change his identity on various burglary jobs. Well educated, with some knowledge of works of art. Known to the American police, so transferred his operations abroad. Acquainted in England with known criminals Rodney Ryder, Jessica Ryder, and Ben Egly.'" The inspector glanced up. "Shall I go on, Mr. Hazard? Or will you?"

Ryder called out shrilly, "If he won't talk, I will!" Kerr silenced him.

"Very well," Hazard growled. "I have excellent connections in the United States among—er—persons who can resell paintings in cities scattered all over the world—mainly in South America, and in Russia via the Asian route."

"Do you mean," the inspector interrupted, "that these persons would sell paintings you stole in England, to wealthy buyers on the other side of the world?"

Hazard said blandly, "That is correct, sir. To this end, I studied up on English painting and planned which ones I wished to take. I made New York my base of operations, and from there, I raised money for this trip, hired my three English friends, assembled my tools, got my passport—"

"A forged passport," the inspector corrected him. "And no doubt a few disguises." Hazard nodded. "Go on."

"Then I had a stroke of luck," Hazard said. "I saw an item in a New York newspaper saying that Martha Logan, the well-known historical novelist, would soon visit the private Carewe Museum in England.

So I made it my business to be aboard the same plane as Mrs. Logan." He smiled faintly in her direction.

Martha leaned forward, frowning and listening.

"It was quite simple to manage," Hazard said. "In order to find out the airline, date, hour, and flight number on which Mrs. Logan would fly, I telephoned her publisher in New York. I represented myself as a reporter and said I wanted to interview her at take-off, and have my photographer take pictures of her boarding the plane. We made an appointment for an interview, and I was given the flight information. Of course I never showed up for the interview. Instead, I purchased a ticket for myself for the same flight. And then, once aboard the plane, I recognized Martha Logan from her photograph on the jackets of her books."

Martha squirmed. "And then you contrived to worm out of me the date and hour when the Carewe Museum would he opened for me."

"Exactly, my dear lady," Hazard agreed.

"More than that," Martha said in quiet anger, "you found out I was acquainted with the owner of a leading London art gallery. By entertaining me and my nurse at lunch, you connived to have me introduce you to the gallery owner, Pierre Selsam. I suppose it helped you to gain some inside information about how the gallery is operated."

Hazard said, "I don't know what you're talking about."

"Mr. Hazard," said Inspector Forbes, "I shall read you a report from Scotland Yard, whose men have arrested your chauffeur and accomplice, Ben Egly, this afternoon in London. The Interpol dossier on you mentions Egly, as you noticed, and this was of help to the police. Also, these ladies' description of the 'Shah's' chauffeur was of help."

The inspector picked up another page and read: "'Egly stated this afternoon that shortly after Hazard visited the Selsam Gallery with the American ladies, he and Hazard burglarized the gallery during the night.'"

Hazard turned pale but admitted nothing. The inspector continued:

"'The London police have located the rolled-up paintings from the Selsam Gallery, wrapped in three packages, hidden in an East End warehouse where Egly's cousin works, in an unused storage room under a blanket. Police also found there the paintings taken from the Carewe Museum.'" Hazard needed a minute or two to recover from the shock of this news. "What about Egly, Mr. Hazard?"

Hazard said grudgingly that Ben Egly, who lived in London, was skillful with tools and had a practical knowledge of his country's laws, customs, and roads—which Hazard, a foreigner here, needed. "I regard Ben Egly as coarse, ignorant, stupid though shrewd," Hazard said, "but reliable enough if paid well. Not reliable enough to keep his mouth shut with the police....After the Selsam burglary, I told him to keep out of sight and wait for my orders for the next job."

"That was my job," Ryder spoke up. But the inspector directed Hazard to go on. "We'll get to you later, Ryder."

Hazard said that early during his stay in London, he briefed his other two accomplices, young Mr. and Mrs. Ryder. Having read about the rare Shakespearean paintings being assembled at Stratford-upon-Avon, Hazard sent Rodney Ryder there to find out which paintings were the most valuable. Ryder was also to find out whether the paintings could be stolen in Stratford, or from the train en route to Edinburgh, or could more safely be stolen later from the exhibit hall in Edinburgh.

"To think," Peter whispered to Cherry, "that I took him for a simpleton! For just a tennis partner!"

"That accounts for two burglaries you planned," said the inspector to Hazard. "What about the Carewe Museum job?"

"That took careful preparation and timing," Hazard admitted. During his first day or two in London, he said, he saw on television the colorful Shah Liddy, who was an art collector, with his blond young English wife, arriving to visit England for three to four weeks. In less than three weeks the Carewe Museum would be opened to Martha Logan. Wasn't it believable that the Shah and his wife might unexpectedly visit the Carewe Museum? Very well, Hazard decided, he would impersonate the flamboyant Shah. Egly would act as his chauffeur, and Ryder's wife, young and blond, would pose as Lady Liddy. Assuming the identity of the Liddys was a risk—but a worthwhile one. He just had to take his chances that Carewe and the Liddys had never met.

So he instructed Jessica Ryder, who stayed on in London, to go to The Cat and Fiddle Inn near the Carewe Museum, just a few days before the planned theft, using a false name, Meg Greene. She was to study the country roads and terrain around there, where to abandon a traceable car, how to make the fastest getaway, and other information. On her solitary walks she sketched a map of roads and woods for Mr. Hazard, made a duplicate for Egly, and mailed the maps to Egly in London.

With his plans set in motion, Hazard had left London right after burglarizing the Selsam Gallery. He went to an obscure seaside resort, to think out the details of the Carewe plan, and to wait while the Ryders did their jobs.

Rodney Ryder reported back to him that it would be impossible to steal the Shakespearean paintings in Stratford or from the train; they would have to be stolen in Edinburgh. Hazard then sent Ryder to Edinburgh, to find a hideout for them, and a go-between.

The inspector addressed Ryder. "You telephoned from here to your wife at The Cat and Fiddle Inn, rather than phoning this information to Hazard—is that correct?"

"Yes, sir," Ryder said. "Because Hazard had returned to London and was keeping under cover. My wife relayed it to him."

In London, Hazard said under questioning, he rented a black Bentley as discreetly as possible, and obtained a false driver's license. He bought disguising clothes, a white wig, and a false white beard for himself, some appropriate garments for Jessica Ryder, and a chauffeur's uniform for Ben Egly. Egly, using a false name and a false driver's license, bought for cash a secondhand, inconspicuous old sedan and changed its license plates. In this way Egly left no leads for the police later to trace the old sedan, which was to be the getaway car.

By now Jessica Ryder's maps arrived. Hazard had already instructed her to meet him on a deserted road at nine thirty on the morning of the projected theft.

"Egly and I left London the day before the Carewe job," Hazard said. "I wore my usual clothes, with a hat and sunglasses, and drove the Bentley. Egly was dressed as a workman and he drove the old sedan."

"Yes, the Windermere police have reported that you apparently drove all day, traveling separately," the inspector said, consulting another report. "And you and Egly stayed overnight, separately, at two of the lodging-houses along the highway."

"Well, no one noticed us," Hazard said with satisfaction. "Next morning we each started out early, and separately. Ben Egly drove the old sedan into the woods, put on the chauffeur's uniform, and waited. I picked up Jessica Ryder on the road, in the Bentley, and we joined Egly in the woods. That's where I put on the 'Shah's' clothing and beard. Jessica changed from 'Meg Greene's' tweed suit into 'Lady Liddy's' fine clothes. And then—" Hazard shrugged.

"Then the theft went off smoothly as planned," the inspector supplied. "You abandoned the Bentley, and changed out of your disguises. I presume, Mr. Hazard, that Egly concealed the stolen Carewe paintings in the old sedan and drove them to London?" Hazard nodded. "And you traveled alone to Edinburgh?"

"The three of us scattered," Hazard said, "since the police would be looking for a couple and another man."

"Archie, if you tell where my wife is," Ryder burst out, "I'll make you regret it! Sooner or later!"

"Mr. Ryder," said Inspector Forbes, "it will go easier for you if you tell us where she is."

Cherry, Martha, and Peter watched Ryder as he hesitated, nervously biting his lips. "I can't do it," he said.

"Mr. Hazard, you will cooperate and tell us," the inspector directed.

"Well, Egly drove the sedan south toward London. I—I figured the police could hardly suspect a workman driving an old car of having the Carewe treasures," Hazard hedged. He avoided Ryder's burning look. "Jessica Ryder was sitting on the floor in the back of the sedan so that she wouldn't be seen. I'm not really sure where she—if she—"

"Get on with it, Hazard!" the inspector commanded.

"Egly was to let her out at Lancaster, the nearest big town," Hazard said in a low voice. "From there she was to take a train to her mother's house in—" He named a Midlands city as Sergeant Kerr restrained Rodney Ryder from hitting the older man.

The sergeant moved Ryder to a chair on the opposite side of the room. Inspector Forbes resumed:

"Describe your movements after the theft, Mr. Hazard."

"Well, I was dressed as myself again, and I left the woods on foot," Hazard said. "I walked behind hedges down a country road, to where Jessica had told me I could hail a bus, at one of its pickup points. I changed to another bus at the nearest town, and kept changing buses and trains so that nobody would have much chance to notice me. I reached Edinburgh late Monday evening." Hazard said regretfully, "Except that my wrenched ankle was beginning to swell and bother me, our plan was working out on schedule. I went to 26 Weir Street where Rod was waiting for me and—well, you probably know the rest."

"We know," said the inspector. "Mr. Ryder, we will interrogate you later, privately. Both of you will be flown to London, under arrest. You 'enterprising art collectors' can now look forward to trials and prison terms."

The inspector asked the Americans if there were anything they wished to add to Hazard's statements. They did not, but Cherry had a question:

"What will become of Amy?"

"The shopwoman's ten-year-old daughter?" The inspector looked thoughtful. "We never suspected a child, did we? I expect that that unfortunate child will be taken away from her mother, and placed in the custody of foster parents who are fit to raise her."

"I understand from Mrs. Kirby's neighbors, sir," said Sergeant Kerr, "that Amy has grandparents and an aunt, on her deceased father's side, who are good people."

Inspector Forbes said he was glad to hear that. So was Cherry. Martha and Peter looked relieved, too.

"Another constructive fact," said the inspector, "is that a third art theft has been prevented. I wish to thank our visitors for their role in that." Hazard snorted. The inspector said to the guards, "Take the prisoners out."

Hazard was taken out one door, and Ryder, glowering at him, was hustled out the other door. Most of the detectives left except Mr. Cox and Mr. Kerr, who came to ask Cherry if she were quite all right.

"I'm fine again, thanks," Cherry said. "Thank you for rescuing me."

Inspector Forbes held out his hand to the visitors. Cherry said, "I wish Auntie Pru could receive a medal or something else spectacular."

The inspector looked amused. "Let's say she will receive the equivalent of an honorable mention in the newspaper reports."

They all said goodbye. Peter escorted Martha and Cherry out of the building, and hailed a taxi. He suggested dinner together, but Martha said she and Cherry had better have a quiet dinner in their rooms, and go right to sleep. It was late, and even Peter admitted they all had had enough for one day.

"But may I meet you both tomorrow morning?" Peter asked. "Tomorrow's my last day here."

"It's a date," Cherry said, and Martha said, "Let's not go chasing any thieves."

The next day was sunny and fine. They drove up the historic rock to where Edinburgh Castle perched two hundred and seventy feet in the air. The rock fell sharply on three sides, a natural fortress. As they toured the castle, Peter paid more attention to Cherry than to the guide whom Martha Logan had engaged. The castle had a long, bloody history, said the guide. He took them into the stone-walled apartments where Mary, Queen of Scots, had lived, and into a very small stone room where she bore her son, James VI, who became King James I of England. They traveled still further back into time and history when they stepped into the plain, stony, little Norman chapel where Queen Margaret, who became Saint Margaret, had prayed during the wars and sieges of the eleventh century. On the altar were a few fresh roses, white and red, as if the lady herself had set them there while the castle was being captured and recaptured. Indeed, the guide said, the origins of the castle were lost in antiquity, but went back to the Bronze Age.

Then they crossed the open courtyard to visit the beautiful National War Memorial. Here, in quiet grandeur, were recorded the names of soldiers, and of nurses, Cherry noted, and working people, and even animals who had died in World War I in defense of their country. Feeling subdued, they went outdoors and stood near the barracks, looking down at the city. The guide pointed out to them the Royal Mile, which leads from the castle to Holyrood Palace. Cutting across the heart of Edinburgh lay Princes Street, with its elegant shops and teashops on one side; and on the other, its gardens, monuments, stately churches, and national art museums. "And there," the guide pointed out at the far end of Princes Street, "is your hotel, at the Waverly Steps."

They left the castle. Peter had to pack, but since Martha wanted to shop, he took her and Cherry as far as Princes Street.

Peter did not want to say goodbye. But he had to, "Right here and now, darn it. We have to fly back to the United States today," he said, "if my students and I are to arrive on time for the opening of the fall semester." He looked longingly at Cherry. "I don't suppose you're leaving today, too?"

Cherry smiled and shook her head. Martha answered. "No, we're going to see a little more of Scotland, the lochs and moors and the Robert Burns country. Then we'll fly back to London, and from there fly to New York. Ah—excuse me. I want to send some butterscotch to my children." She started to move away. "I'll join you in half an hour at our hotel, Cherry....Yes, yes, I'll be perfectly all right by myself!"

So Cherry and Peter had a last, short walk together. Peter unashamedly held her hand.

"For once I can't think of an appropriate quotation," he said. "Do you think we'll ever meet again?"

"Well, a nurse moves around a great deal on various assignments," Cherry said.

"Sometimes professors transfer from one college to another," Peter said. "There are vacations—and long weekends—Wait! I haven't your home address."

They wrote down their addresses for each other. "Here's hoping," said Peter. "Here's to travel."

"And no more art thefts," Cherry said.

They walked a while in silence. They reached the hotel and paused. Still Peter held fast to her hand. "I'd like to give you something to remember me by," he said. "A souvenir bracelet—or a book of Robert Burns's poems?"

Cherry gently wriggled her hand free. "Thanks anyway, Peter. I'll remember you, all right, without any souvenir. Just telephone me long-distance some time and see if I don't."

"I will!" said Peter. "So help me, I will!"

"It's been nice. So long for now," said Cherry.

In case you missed *Cherry Ames, Staff Nurse* ...

~~~~~~

CHAPTER I

The Young Volunteers

IN THE KITCHEN CHERRY HELPED HERSELF TO A TASTE OF the potato salad she and her mother had just made for the cookout. Today had been a hot, joyous Fourth of July, and by now, five-thirty P.M., Cherry had worked up quite an appetite. Mrs. Ames saw her and smilingly shook her head.

"Cherry, you and your brother Charles always were great ones for 'tasting' every dish before it came to the table. If I don't stop you, there'll be a large hole in that platter of potato salad. What are we going to do with her, Velva?"

Velva, the young farm woman who helped Mrs. Ames, laughed comfortably. "Oh, I'll make us another batch of potato salad if we run short," she said.

"I don't think we'll run short on anything," Cherry said, looking at the heaped-up platters of deviled eggs and salads and the big chocolate cake Velva had baked.

Just looking at these made Cherry hungrier than before. "Shall I take some of these platters out to the yard now, Mother?"

Edith Ames glanced at the kitchen clock. "Well, Charles should be back with the ice cream any minute now. Yes, take them out, dear. Velva and I still have to finish making the iced tea."

Cherry filled a tray with as many platters as she could carry at one time, and went out of the house. It was a big, old-fashioned house with a spacious yard and shade trees. At the rear of the yard, a safe distance away from Mrs. Ames's cherished flower garden, a streamer of smoke rose from the brick grill Mr. Ames had built. He and young Dr. Dan Blake were working to get a charcoal fire burning.

Cherry grinned at their attire. Her father sported a chef's cap and apron. Dr. Dan wore a brightly, wildly patterned sports shirt over his trousers, probably in reaction to the whites he wore all week at Hilton Hospital. Dr. Blake was a new young M.D. from Colorado; for a year now he had been in this neighborly, middle-sized town of Hilton, Illinois. As a resident physician, he both worked and lived at the hospital, but this rather isolated him and he was a little lonesome on his first job. Cherry often saw Dr. Dan outside the hospital, as well as during her duty hours on Women's Orthopedics. She was glad her family liked Dan, too.

"Hi, you chefs!" Cherry called.

Dr. Dan Blake turned, flushed from the heat of the grill. "Here, let me give you a hand—" He came to take her tray, and carried it to the picnic table. "Mm, look at all the home cooking!"

Cherry smiled up at him. Dr. Dan had the same dark crisp hair and vivid coloring as Cherry; in a way he looked more like her than her blond twin brother did. "We expect you to do justice to our home cooking," she said.

Dr. Dan smiled back. "I just hope you like the way I grill beefburgers. Of course your dad is the master chef."

Mr. Ames shoved back his chef's cap and mopped his forehead. "I am a real-estate man pretending to be a cook, and not doing very well at it," he said. "Come back here, Dr. Dan. I need you."

Cherry set out the platters of food on the picnic table and returned to the kitchen to reload the tray. When she came outdoors again, Charlie drove up and parked the car in front of the house. A gallon container of ice cream sat beside him on the front seat. He got out of the car with it and called to Cherry:

"I'm starving! When do we eat?"

"Well, Dr. Fortune and Midge aren't here yet," Cherry said.

"I saw Midge talking to some kids on the next block. Maybe she's on her way here," Charlie said, and disappeared into the house.

Midge probably was trying to do her share, Cherry thought, in recruiting teenage volunteers to work in the hospital this summer. Extra help was badly needed in all hospitals, and especially in Hilton Hospital. It had no nursing school, hence no student nurses to help the overworked R.N.'s. Every one of its three hundred beds was now occupied, and every one of the hospital's many departments needed helpers. The hospital's limited budget required volunteers. With summer, most of the adult volunteers were going off on vacations with their families; they *had* to be replaced.

Last summer Hilton Hospital had tried out, in a small way, training a few junior volunteers. Midge Fortune had been one of the Jayvees then, and that was why she was such an enthusiastic recruiter now. Last summer's experiment had shown that the youngsters could bring real help and uplifting spirits to the hospital. The program had petered out over the winter when the teenagers had been busy with schoolwork.

Well, that often happened, Cherry thought. She hoped Midge, in her enthusiasm, would not invite anyone too young. The American Hospital Association required that a junior volunteer must be at least fourteen to serve in the hospital. To be a ward aide, and work with the nurses and patients, the junior must be at least sixteen.

Cherry walked across the lawn to see whether the chefs needed an assistant. They did not; everything was ready. Mr. Ames sat down on the picnic bench and helped himself and Dr. Dan to a "sample" of potato salad, while they waited for the Fortunes.

"How's your schedule coming along?" Dr. Dan asked Cherry. "Wish I had some way to help you."

"Thanks. It'll work out," Cherry said.

At her head nurse's request, she had been figuring out a temporary schedule—a schedule by which she could teach some of the incoming juniors, and still do her full share of nursing for her patients. Cherry had offered to teach, since she had already done so the previous summer.

Midge came running into the Ames's yard. "Hi, you kids!" she said. She hugged Mr. Ames, grinned at Cherry and Dr. Dan, and popped a pickle into her mouth.

Midge was practically a member of the Ames family. Her father, Dr. Joe Fortune, had been the Ames's doctor from the time Cherry and Charlie were born. Midge's mother had died when the girl was little, and she had grown up as much in the Ames's house as in her own. She was sixteen now. She pushed her light-brown hair off her moist forehead and said:

"Whew! I got three more promises—Oh, before I forget! My father said to tell you he's pretty tired from watching the parade with me this morning and treating an emergency case this afternoon, so would you all please excuse him if he comes over later? He's taking a nap now."

The others nodded. Dr. Joe was not very strong. Cherry said she had better tell her mother and Velva, so the cookout could begin now. The two chefs very seriously put the first round of beefburgers on the grill.

Midge followed Cherry across the yard. "I got promises from two more girls and a boy," Midge announced.

Cherry smiled. "Good for you. Relax, now. You don't have to do the whole recruiting job single-handed."

The high school and the junior high school had cooperated with the hospital in initiating the Jayvee program. Cherry did not want to deflate Midge's enthusiasm by reminding her that all during the last weeks of school—final examinations notwithstanding—the teacher-sponsors and the Jayvee announcements on the school bulletin board had awakened a lively response. Another effective means had been that radio disk jockey's appeal for Jayvees. It had brought in so many immediate telephoned inquiries that the hospital switchboard had lighted up as if disaster calls were coming in. Some of the doctors and nurses did think the juniors were going to be a disaster. Some of the youngsters' parents had their doubts, too, and parents' written permission was needed to become a Jayvee.

"Anyway, you have to remember," Cherry said, to Midge, "that all the promises so far are only from *prospective* Jayvees. Some of these eager beavers will tour the hospital next Monday, and decide that hospital work is not for them. Some of them won't even show up for the tour."

Midge protested, but Cherry insisted.

"Another thing," Cherry said. "Miss Vesey, our Director of Volunteers, won't find that *every* applicant is the right person to work in a hospital. She says she has to discourage a number of applicants, grownups, even, because they're either not right for hospital work, or they may be overconfident, or else they're so shy that they're not much help."

"We'll do better than that," Midge said stoutly.

"You'll see," said Cherry. "Come help me carry out the iced tea."

Mrs. Ames was sorry to learn that Dr. Fortune felt so tired, but said he could have his supper whenever he came. Charlie helped the two girls bring out the rest of the dishes, Velva and Mrs. Ames followed, and all but Dr. Dan sat down at the picnic table. He insisted on being the one to serve the beefburgers since, as Mr. Ames conceded, he had prepared them.

"Delicious!" everyone said, and Velva said, "Better'n the ones I make." Dr. Dan was so pleased that he flushed. There was not much conversation during supper; everybody was busy eating. Charlie amiably offered to grill the second round of beefburgers, but—rather to his relief—Dr. Dan was voted master chef. The smell of charcoal smoke mingled with the fresh fragrance of flowers and grass. The sun dropped, and long shadows stretched across the yard. By the time the seven of them had enjoyed Velva's cake, it was evening.

"Will you sing for us, Dr. Dan?" said Mrs. Ames. "I hope you brought your guitar."

He had left it in his car, parked at the curb. "Just in case no one wanted to be pestered with my singing," he remarked. Now he brought the guitar to the picnic table. Striking a chord, Dr. Dan looked at Cherry and said:

"What would you like?"

"'Wabash Blues,'" said Cherry and Charlie in the same breath. The Wabash River flowed eight miles from here.

"'My Indiana Home,'" said Velva, who came from the state of Indiana just across the Wabash.

Mrs. Ames asked for "Home on the Range." Mr. Ames requested a spiritual. Dr. Dan sang them all, and sang them well. Neighbors strolling past paused to listen.

The moon came out. In the Ames's house the telephone rang and Mrs. Ames went to answer it. She came back outdoors and said:

"That was your father, Midge. He said he just woke up, isn't presentable, and isn't ambitious enough to come over. We'll pack up a picnic lunch for him and somebody will take it to him."

"We'll all go," said Cherry.

As soon as Velva had the picnic basket ready, Cherry, Midge, Dr. Dan, and Charlie all piled into Dr. Dan's car. First stop was the Fortunes' cottage. Then they went for a cooling drive through Lincoln Park. Late as it was, the excitement of a big holiday still filled the town.

Dr. Dan said in a low voice to Cherry, "I'd hoped we could go off for a drive by ourselves this evening. Guess I sang for too long."

"Never mind," said Cherry. "The summer is just beginning."

The rest of that first week in July was hot, even for corn growing country. After a slow, hot weekend, Cherry was glad to be back at work in the hospital on

Monday morning. She came in at seven-thirty A.M., half an hour earlier than usual, to allow herself time for the Jayvee tour later that morning.

As she stood in uniform in the main corridor waiting for the elevator, an orderly who worked in Emergency came up. He was wheeling a high stretcher on which a young woman lay with knees and wrists in odd, stiff positions. The patient was dressed in night clothes and robe. She was conscious but dazed—probably with pain, Cherry thought.

The orderly motioned Cherry aside and said in a low voice:

"I'm taking this young lady to your ward, Nurse Ames. Dr. Blake saw her just now—on Emergency—rheumatoid arthritis attack—said he'll be up on Orthopedics right away."

"Thanks," Cherry said, and with her lips silently formed the question, "Medication?" The orderly said, "Aspirin." Cherry bent over the young woman to reassure her. Even with her face screwed up in pain she was pretty, with soft brown hair and velvety dark-brown eyes, and almost as small as a child. She looked up at Cherry and gasped out:

"Nurse, I don't want to be an invalid! I'm afraid!"

"You won't be disabled," Cherry said. "You're young enough to get well. And we're going to give you all the right medication and treatment. Rest, now."

"There's no known cure for arthritis, my doctor said so!" The young woman's dark eyes filled with tears. "Look, I can't move my wrists or my knees. Swollen stiff. They hurt so! I can't walk! I'll—I'll spend the rest of my life in a wheelchair—"

Cherry knew that arthritis made its sufferers pessimistic and often emotionally dependent. She said kindly but firmly, "Don't be frightened. We're here to help you."

The patient had not heard a word Cherry said. She cried all the way upstairs. Cherry dismissed the orderly, and aided by the ward's alerted night nurse, transferred the patient to a prepared bed. She tried to hide her wet face in the pillow. The other women patients, awake in their beds, watched in silence. Some of them, Cherry realized, were pretty discouraged themselves; she wished a few young Jayvees were here to distract them.

Dr. Dan Blake came in at once. He smiled at Cherry and Mrs. Page, the night nurse, as he handed them the admitting interviewer's notes, then went over to talk softly to the new patient.

Cherry and the night nurse read together: "Wilmot, Margaret (Peggy). 1617 Lincoln Drive, Hilton. Age twenty-six. Widow, no relatives near. Brought in ambulance by Dr. Fairall who treated her two weeks ago for a severe strep throat. Dr. Fairall stated impossible to foresee that infection would move from strep throat into blood stream and into joints, causing acute rheumatoid arthritis. Sudden explosive attack early this A.M. with temperature of 103. Weakness, fatigue, recent loss of weight, now very painful swollen red wrists and knees. Patient incapacitated, alone, barely able to telephone doctor."

"Poor thing," Cherry murmured.

"I should say so," the night nurse murmured back. "If you'd like me to stay on after eight o'clock, I can. I hear you're going to be busy with teenagers this morning."

"Thanks, but you've put in a long night's work," Cherry said to Mrs. Page. "If necessary, the juniors will have to wait, or Miss Vesey will take charge of them."

Peggy Wilmot had stopped crying. The young doctor motioned Cherry and Ethel Page into the hall, to the nurses' station outside the ward door, where the patients could not overhear—and worry.

"Well"—Dr. Dan Blake stopped smiling—"this new case looks plenty serious, but she will not require surgery. Of course for a definitive examination and orders, we'll have to see what Dr. Watson says when he comes in." Dr. Ray Watson was the senior doctor in charge of all Orthopedic wards. "He'll want to consult with Dr. Fairall. In the meantime," Dr. Dan Blake said, "we'll support those inflamed wrists and knees with splints, and give her all the comfort measures we can. Mrs. Page, please bring me four aluminum splints. Cherry—I mean, Miss Ames—I'd like you to work with me."

"Yes, Doctor," Cherry said. She did try, at work, to forget that they were friends after working hours.

Peggy Wilmot had fallen asleep. Cherry gently woke her so she would not be startled when Dr. Blake applied the splints. He explained to her that the lightweight "gutter" splints, open on top, would support the inflamed joints of her wrists and knees.

"First of all, Mrs. Wilmot, you must rest these inflamed joints," he said. "Moving your wrists and knees will cause pain. The splints will immobilize them and also hold them in normal positions, so that when the inflammation subsides, you won't be left with any deformity."

Peggy Wilmot winced with pain as Dr. Blake adjusted the splints that Mrs. Page brought. "I won't be deformed, will I?" she asked.

"No, you won't," Dr. Dan said. "Now why are you looking so worried? Don't you trust your doctors and nurses?"

He threw Cherry a look that said, "You'll have to reassure her and get rid of this worry of hers." Cherry nodded. The patient's attitude had a great deal to do with getting well.

By the time four splints were applied, with light sandbags placed against the splints to increase the corrective force, the night nurse had left and the daytime staff had come in.

The head nurse, Miss Julia Greer, came over to welcome the new patient. Confidence exuded from Miss Greer's trim, erect figure, and kindness shone in her lined, intelligent face. Cherry never had worked with a more superlative nurse than Julia Greer; the entire hospital respected and loved this woman who had devoted a lifetime to it. Some of her strength came across to Peggy Wilmot, who smiled for the first time this morning.

And after Cherry had given her the additional aspirin Dr. Blake prescribed, and the other daytime nurse, Mary Corsi, had come over to say hello to young Mrs. Wilmot, and Cherry had washed her face, she said:

"You're all so kind to me. I wish you'd call me Peggy."

"Peggy it is," said Cherry. "Now how would you like some breakfast?"

It was necessary to feed the helpless patient gently, without hurry. She ate gratefully, dependently. She reminded Cherry of a child, a small, scared child.

Morning care and breakfast for the other patients took up Cherry's time until Dr. Ray Watson came in on his morning rounds. He came booming and stomping in, an abundantly good-humored elderly man, and the entire ward perked up.

Cherry wanted to stay to hear his prognosis and what drugs he ordered for the new patient, but Miss Julia Greer whispered to her:

"The Director of Volunteers telephoned just now that you'd better come down right away. She says there's a small, enthusiastic mob of juniors, and that several of them are asking for you."

"But I want to hear about Mrs. Wilmot—"

"Come back at lunchtime, my dear, and I'll tell you. You've done all anyone can for her, for now. Getting help from the juniors is important, too."

Cherry thanked her. She righted her starched cap on her dark curls, and hurried off to the brand-new Hospitality Lounge, a room especially prepared for the juniors.

A bright paper banner, lettered WELCOME JUNIORS, stretched across one wall of the Hospitality Lounge. Some fifty young people waited here. Because they were in a hospital, they were unaccustomedly quiet. Cherry noticed that the girls outnumbered the boys three or four to one. Up at the front of the room, chatting with the youngsters, were Mrs. Streeter, the Superintendent of Nurses, with Dr. Joe Fortune, and one or two white-clad nurses. Apparently Mr. Howe, the Hospital Administrator, and Dr. Keller, the Medical Superintendent, were too busy to attend, but they had given their permission for a Jayvee program, along with the high school and junior high school principals, and that was the main thing. Cherry started toward the front of the room but was quickly surrounded by boys and girls.

"Remember me, Miss Cherry? I'm Dorothy Ware— Dodo." A bouncy, giggly, plump girl pumped Cherry's hand. "Can I please work with you on Orthopedics, please? Midge thinks maybe I can."

"We'll see, Dodo," Cherry said.

Midge was acting very important and proud because, except for two other girls, she was the only experienced Jayvee here. Cherry waved to the other two. One was lanky, droll Emma Weaver who loved to cook. The other was Carol Nichols, who seemed older than fifteen; she had a knack for drawing and she was dependable. Cherry had heard that the other few former Jayvees had gone away on vacations with their families.

A quiet, dark, studious-looking boy of about fourteen or fifteen said to Cherry, "I'm Myron Stern. This is my friend, Dave McNeil." Dave was tall, strapping, rosy, about fifteen.

Cherry shook hands with both boys. "I'm sure the hospital will be glad to have you."

Myron Stern looked embarrassed. "You know, at school they gave physical examinations to those of us who want to be volunteers. Seems I have a slight heart murmur. I never knew about it before. That won't rule me out, will it? I'm perfectly well and strong, otherwise."

His friend Dave McNeil said, "You're good at lab work. Maybe they'll let you help out in one of the hospital labs. How about that, Miss Ames?"

"I don't see why not," Cherry said. "We wouldn't allow Myron to be a messenger, but the labs could use a clerk." She explained that supervisors decided which assignments went to volunteers. "But don't worry, the supervisors will try to honor your request if they possibly can."

"Thanks, Miss Ames," both boys said. Dave called after her, laughing, "I'd like a nice cool job in the Pharmacy's refrigerator this summer."

Cherry grinned and then her grin faded as a tall, beautiful, overdressed blond girl seized her hand.

"Oh, I'm so happy to meet you, Miss Cherry! I'm Lillian Jones. I do so hope the hospital will accept me! I think it would be just wonderful to serve here." Her mascaraed eyes held a faraway gleam.

The girl was a born actress, Cherry thought in amusement, who saw herself in the role of ministering angel.

Still, Lillian might just turn out to be serious about volunteer work. Cherry said something encouraging and moved on.

One person she was glad to see here was Bud Johnson. She knew this freckled, sturdily built boy from the Orthopedic wards where he had worked last summer as an orderly, and she knew Bud to be solidly dependable, like a rock. He said "Hi!" to Cherry, as one professional to another, and went on talking confidently to three girls who looked uncertain but impressed. Cherry answered "Hi," and pushed her way ahead, past the taller, quieter seventeen- and eighteen-year-old girls, to the staff persons in white.

Cherry said good morning to Mrs. Streeter and to Midge's father, Dr. Fortune. He was having an argument—as far as anyone so gentle would argue—with a skinny, eyeglassed woman in white who seemed to bristle. She was Mrs. Jenkins, Head Nurse of the Women's Medical Ward, and she was asserting:

"Suppose a junior volunteer makes a mistake? I say, keep them in the linen room. Kids have no place on the wards."

"And did an adult never make a mistake, Mrs. Jenkins?" Dr. Fortune answered. "I know some youngsters who are more reliable than some adults. All these young persons here today have good scholastic and character records. They have the idealism to want to help others."

"Humph!" Mrs. Jenkins said. "They like the uniform better than the job." Then she had to keep quiet, because Mrs. Streeter was calling the meeting to order.

The teenagers listened soberly as Dr. Fortune and then the Superintendent of Nurses each made a brief address. Dr. Fortune said: "Hospital work is hard work. It is literally life-and-death work. Your only reward will be the satisfaction of helping others. However, if you are planning a career in medicine or nursing—if you like people and want to learn more about them—or if you simply want to do something really needed and important, the hospital welcomes you."

Mrs. Streeter spoke of the shortage of nurses—so urgent that the ward nurses had barely enough time to give essential services to their patients. "Particularly," she said, "we don't have time to give a patient the extra attentions and individual interest he needs to encourage him to get well. Besides, there are dozens of other vital jobs—every bit as urgent as nursing—where we need your extra hands and tireless legs to keep this hospital functioning."

There were several rules to observe. Miss Ann Vesey, the attractive, friendly young Director of Volunteers, who did not look much older than a teenager herself, explained the rules. Junior volunteers would not participate in medication and treatment of patients. All volunteers of any age would be under close professional supervision. Any person who worked in the Food Services Department or in the Pediatrics Ward or playroom with children must have chest X-rays and frequent throat cultures taken. In some states the teenagers would have to obtain working papers, but this was not true in Illinois. The hospital would train

the volunteers in a general class and then on the teenagers' specific jobs.

"Since there is so much to do, and so few of us to
do it," Miss Vesey said, "we recommend that most,
if not all, of you serve in more than one department.
Having two assignments will give you an interesting
change of pace, and more experience, too."

After fifty hours of service, the juniors would receive
award pins, at an evening party to which they and their
parents would be invited. There was a little stir of pleasure at that.

Bud Johnson raised his hand. "What hours do you
want us here?"

Miss Vesey said that juniors in other hospitals found
that two or three full days a week worked out well for
them and for the hospitals. "That's a seven-hour day,
or you can volunteer for half days if you'd rather," she
said. "No night work."

The Director of Volunteers announced the teenagers would tour the hospital. They would see for themselves where and how they were needed. The tour
would help them decide what assignments to volunteer for, or whether to volunteer at all.

"Ask questions if you like, but very quietly, so the
patients won't hear you. Please don't touch anything."

Miss Vesey, with Cherry and another R.N. to help
with explanations, led the large group first to the
Out-Patient Clinic, on the ground floor. In this big
room, with booths, sat all kinds of patients; doctors

and interviewers studied their records, talked to them. Jayvees—older ones—were very much needed here to take the patients' laboratory reports to—or records from—the Records Room; to take the patients' temperatures and to weigh them; to escort patients, some in wheelchairs, to X-ray or some special medical department.

Cherry said to the juniors near her, "You'll work with the clinic social worker, compile new charts, answer phones." Some of the teenagers looked interested, others apprehensive.

Everyone regained confidence when they came to the Medical Records Room. What could be so difficult about filing? But Miss Vesey said, "There are thousands of records in here. If you misfile one, good-bye record! When a report comes down from a lab or X-ray, you *must* file it on the proper patient's charts—imagine what a mistake could lead to!" Only carefully selected Jayvees were trusted to work in here.

The group skipped Emergency, which, like Surgical, contagious wards, and the Maternity floor upstairs, was off limits to them. They had a look at the Admitting Office, where Jayvee's escort service was needed. They went on to the Pharmacy, which was interesting with its supplies of medicine. Mr. Cox, registered graduate pharmacist, was in charge. Cherry overheard some boys in back of her say, "Pharmacy for us!" Cherry turned around and said, "Fair warning, fellows. Good jobs and dull jobs, *all* must he done. Everyone must do half and half, though we will try to meet your interests."

The girls, when the group went upstairs, all wanted to help on the children's wards and in the playroom. Small patients, some kneeling in their cribs, some clumsily feeding themselves at tiny tables, shyly waved back to the teenagers. A small boy on miniature crutches came up to Dodo Ware and asked, "Play with me?"

Into several convalescent wards, Medical and Surgical, past rows of beds, went the teenagers. Cherry made it a point to notice which juniors smiled at the patients, and which ones simply stared.

The group went to the X-ray Department, with its many records to take care of, then on to the big Pathology Laboratory where the white-coated technologist in charge said, "We certainly need helpers to wash test tubes and run errands." Next, they went to Central Sterile Supply where Emma Weaver remarked, "The sterilizers look like giant pressure cookers."

In here, juniors were needed to wash and pack sterilized rubber gloves, sponges, wooden tongue depressors. Green packages went to Surgical, yellow to Maternity, white for general use.

"What boring work!" Lillian Jones sighed.

The woman in charge heard her and turned around. "Young lady, sterile or not is a matter of life or death. Infection will be spread if this job isn't done properly."

That sobered everybody. Some of the teenagers looked still more shaken when, out in the hall, they came smack up against an iron lung, to be sent upstairs to a polio patient, and oxygen tents waiting for calls for them.

Cherry said, "I was scared to pieces, too, when I was just starting out as a student nurse. You get over it with training."

Some of the teenagers murmured, "Thanks." Some of them limped a little, after the long tour, on their way back to the Hospitality Lounge. There everyone stood about uncertainly. Cherry glanced at her wristwatch. She was growing impatient to go back to her ward and the new patient.

The Director of Volunteers said, "If any of you want to volunteer right now, you may do so. Some of you may prefer to go home and talk over with your parents whether being a hospital aide is for you. Tomorrow morning we'll meet here again at ten. Then after you take a pledge of service, you can volunteer for assignments of your choice. Be prepared to stay tomorrow— we have a big program ahead for you. Thank you all for coming today. Good morning."

A few of the young people slipped away. Several stayed to ask questions. Cherry was sorry she could not stay on, but her patients were waiting for her. She waved to Midge and Bud and several others, and went back upstairs.

The head nurse met her hurrying into the ward. Cherry said, "I think I'll skip lunch hour, Miss Greer, and catch up on my work. How is the new patient?"

"Better have some lunch, Miss Ames," said Miss Greer. "Miss Corsi and I doubled up on the few morning chores you didn't have time to finish. No, don't say thank you! Your new patient is resting a little more comfortably.

She seems anxious about one thing—she asked for her mail. Someone will have to bring it from her house."

"Asked for her mail? As sick as she is!" Cherry said. "Must be mighty important mail."

"Well, I don't want her upset," the head nurse said, "by mail or anything else." Cherry knew that with arthritics, emotional stress could cause a physical setback or bring on an attack. "Her mail can wait until tomorrow," Miss Greer said.

"By tomorrow I'll have a junior volunteer who'll go pick it up," Cherry said, and thought of sending Midge.

Cherry obediently ate some lunch, quickly, leaving a few minutes' free time to go see her new patient. Peggy Wilmot was half asleep but murmured something. Cherry bent over her.

"In my wallet—a check—please cash it for me—" Peggy got out. "I've had it in my wallet since last week. I—I felt so sick I didn't go to the bank."

"You needn't worry about money just yet, or about anything—"

But Peggy insisted, and her face screwed up in anxiety and pain. Cherry did not argue. She promised to ask the woman in the Admitting Office, which kept patients' belongings under lock and key, to bring Peggy her wallet. Peggy would then endorse the check, as best she could, and Cherry would cash it for her. It was a small favor, if it would quiet the patient.

Peggy Wilmot looked so relieved, so grateful, that Cherry wondered why all this strong feeling about her mail and a check.

CHAPTER II

Off to a Good Start

TUESDAY WAS PLEDGE DAY. AT A LITTLE BEFORE TEN, Cherry finished up two hours' work on her ward; she had just carefully changed Peggy Wilmot's position and applied dry heat, both as comfort measures. That was as much nursing as she could do for Peggy, until later today. So Cherry went downstairs and gave her attention to the junior volunteers.

At the front of the Hospitality Lounge, several staff people waited. Cherry said good morning and joined them. She felt rather anxious to see how many young volunteers would actually come. Several teenagers were already here: Midge and freckled Bud Johnson, sitting together—the quiet steady ones; Claire Alison, Carol Nichols with the sketchbook she always carried, Dave McNeil and Myron Stern—two or three young persons whom Cherry did not know by name—and tall, theatrical-looking Lillian Jones, somewhat to Cherry's surprise. Not very many. Cherry would not have blamed any youngster who would rather go swimming in the county fairgrounds pool, this hot July morning. Still, more teenagers came in, self-conscious, determined. Dodo Ware practically bounced in, round eyes shining. By the time Mrs. Streeter rose to speak, she had twenty recruits to greet—fourteen girls and six boys.

"I am glad to see such a good turnout," said the Superintendent of Nurses. "On behalf of the Administrator of this hospital, its doctors and nurses and entire staff, I congratulate you on your high purpose. We are happy to have you join us as part of our team."

Mrs. Streeter said they would not spend much time on ceremonies; there was too much urgent work to be done. She asked the young volunteers to stand, and in chorus they repeated after her this pledge:

"I will be punctual ... immaculately clean ... conscientious ... accept supervision ... not seek information regarding a patient ... make my work professional ... uphold the standards of this hospital and interpret them to the community." Then, and most important, "I will consider as confidential all information which I may hear in this hospital."

The juniors were asked to pledge at least fifty hours' work over this summer. Now they could volunteer for whatever assignments they had their hearts set on. They had been interviewed yesterday afternoon by Miss Vesey, the young Director of Volunteers, and were realistic about what they could and could not ask for. Carol Nichols, who was fifteen, put her hand up first.

"I'd hoped to work in the blood bank and in clinic registration, please," Carol said.

Midge waved her hand enthusiastically. Being sixteen made her eligible to work in the patient areas. "I'd like to volunteer for Women's Orthopedics"—she shot a loyal look at Cherry—"and the X-ray Department." Cherry knew Midge had little interest in doing clerical work in the X-ray Department, but the staff there needed help.

"Me, too!" said Dodo Ware, and looked questioningly toward Cherry.

"I'm delighted to have you both," Cherry said.

Bud Johnson elected to work as an orderly, wherever the hospital needed him. Miss Vesey replied he would be a floater on the various wards. "And how would you like to help out, Bud, with adult and children's recreation? You know, occasional shows and ward parties."

"I'd like that just fine!" Bud said.

Myron Stern realized his wish: he would work in the Pathology Laboratory. Dave McNeil asked for and got assigned to the coveted Pharmacy, with its room-size refrigerator; he would also work in the Records Room. The youngest juniors were assigned to Central Sterile Supply—and also to the children's playroom and to the patients' flower service. Lillian Jones asked for the Reception Desk, and cheerfully accepted a job in the Dietary Kitchen as well.

Others requested special jobs "and wherever else I'm needed." Soon Mrs. Streeter said, "Now you will please go for your uniforms."

Cherry led the fourteen girls to the nurses' locker room where they put on the white cotton, short-sleeved dresses that Hilton Hospital had lent them. The girls themselves had purchased red-and-white candy-striped cotton pinafores with ruffled bibs to wear over the dresses. Getting into the uniform was a big occasion. Cherry wondered how the boys were making out with their white cotton lab coats or tunics and white duck trousers.

When all the girls were in uniform, Cherry said, "You look very nice, except for your feet." All looked down at their feet. "After today," Cherry said, "everyone is to wear flat shoes—white or whatever you own, rubber soles if possible—and white bobby socks. No rings or other jewelry, please, only your wristwatch."

"Aren't we going to wear caps, like the nurses?" Midge asked disappointedly. "Most Jayvees do."

Cherry explained that Hilton Hospital wanted only its nurses to wear caps. "Patients think anyone who wears a cap is a nurse, and we don't want any confusion. Come along, now."

The girls assembled in Room 110 where the boys were already waiting, looking proud but uneasy in their whites. Cherry asked everyone to take seats. She went to the head of the improvised classroom. A hospital bed, table, supply chest, bandages, charts, and some other demonstration articles had been brought in.

"I am going to teach you," Cherry said, "some of the fundamentals such as bedmaking, feeding a patient, taking and charting TPR—that's temperature, pulse, and respiration—and folding bandages. Some of you may not need to know about bedmaking, but you never can tell when you may be called upon to pinch hit."

Bud Johnson said gamely, "The more we know, the better."

Cherry demonstrated these techniques, then had the members of the class practice on one another. They laughed a lot, and made a few blunders, but they learned quickly. This part of their preliminary training took all morning. At lunchtime Cherry announced:

"Now that you're members of the staff, the hospital cafeteria is open to you. Or if you'd rather go home for lunch, you may. Please report back here in an hour."

The class rushed out, eager to share cafeteria tables with physicians, surgeons, nurses, and technologists. Midge led the way, proud of her know-how around the hospital. Cherry felt pretty proud of Midge, herself; she should prove to be a huge help on the ward.

Cherry then went to the east entrance of the hospital where she had an appointment to meet her mother for a few minutes at noon. Mrs. Ames had agreed to cash Peggy Wilmot's check, since Cherry had no time to go to the bank, and junior volunteers were not permitted to handle money.

Her mother was there right on time, looking lovely as usual. She smiled and handed Cherry an envelope containing the cash.

"Oh, Mother, you're a friend in need!" Cherry said. "This will make that poor girl feel better—though I don't understand why she's so excited about money matters just now."

"Well, I hope it will help her, and I hope," said Mrs. Ames, "that the check will be honored. Mr. Alison at the bank required me to add my endorsement, too, to the check. That means if the company issuing the check doesn't honor it, and if your patient can't make good, then I will have to reimburse the bank for that sum. And it's a fairly substantial sum."

"Gosh," said Cherry, "I never thought of that. Not that I'd let *you* get stuck, Mother—I noticed it was a printed check from some business firm, not just a personal check, and drawn on the First National Bank of Chicago, so I thought it was all right."

"Oh, it's probably all right. Don't worry about it. I have to run now, honey," said Edith Ames. "I'm having lunch with my Garden Club ladies at Sue Webb's house."

"Enjoy yourself," Cherry called as her mother went down the hospital path to where she had parked the car. "See you at home."

Cherry went upstairs to give Peggy the cash, and to resume her duties.

The patients on the women's orthopedics ward were having lunch, except for Peggy Wilmot. She was asleep. Miss Greer said to let her sleep a little longer. Cherry went to say hello to Mrs. Davis, who had osteoarthritis, which some old people get as they age. Mrs. Davis had no family. No one but the social worker ever came to visit her. This little old lady had had surgery and had already been in the hospital for rehabilitation for a month; she was expected to remain for a month or two longer. When she got out, she would be able to walk again, but with a permanent limp, and always with some pain. Cherry smiled at her, and Mrs. Davis smiled back.

"Were you a good patient this morning, Mrs. Davis?" Cherry asked. "Did you go for your whirlpool treatment?"

"Yes, and the physical therapist says I'm a whole lot better if I only didn't have to be pushed to the therapy room in that wheelchair!"

Liz Emery said from the next bed, "Mrs. Davis wants a motor on the wheelchair, so she can drive the chair herself. I'll bet she could drive it, too!"

Liz was fourteen, blond and pretty, restless in traction but unfailingly good-tempered. She was here because of a fractured heel, suffered when a horse she was riding bareback threw her and she landed on her foot. Cherry was glad her bed and Mrs. Davis's bed were side by side. Liz was cheerful young company for the lonely patient.

Cherry moved on past Liz's bed to speak to quiet Mrs. Swanson, who had a badly sprained back, then spoke to the patients on the other side of the room. Peggy Wilmot was awake now. Since Nurse Corsi was busy serving lunch trays, Cherry fed her.

"Your check is cashed," Cherry told her and handed her the envelope. "I'll call admitting to send someone up for it, and lock it away for you."

"Oh, thanks! That's good," Peggy sighed.

She looked thin and pale—anemia often accompanied arthritis. "Dr. Watson or Dr. Dan probably has ordered a blood-count test for her," Cherry thought. "She may need a special diet." Aloud Cherry said:

"How do your wrists and knees feel? Is the heat helping?" Hot-water bags and heating pads were applied, gently, to her inflamed joints. Heat increased the blood supply to relieve pain and relax muscles.

"Yes, the heat helps some," Peggy said. "Please, no more food, Miss Cherry. I'm not hungry."

She was still in too much pain to want to eat, Cherry realized. She coaxed a few more spoonfuls of custard into her, let Peggy rest a few minutes, then very gently altered her position in the bed. This was to avoid bed sores and stiffness. Then Cherry gently removed Peggy's splints and washed her red wrists and knees, then reapplied the splints, and tied them on loosely with elastic bandages.

"You won't have to wear these splints for long," Cherry told her. "Soon it'll be for only a few hours a day, and when you're asleep."

"I don't think I'll ever get better," Peggy said dejectedly. "Not ever really well and active again. I have an older cousin who's had arthritis for years, and she's—well, she lives in a wheelchair! How will I ever keep house, alone?"

"Peggy, will you please listen to me?" Cherry looked into her unhappy brown eyes. "Chances are good that you *will* get well. You'll be just as lively as ever. People who have arthritis almost always feel unreasonably pessimistic. It's another sign that you're sick."

Peggy absorbed this information while Cherry glanced at her chart. Dr. Watson had ordered drugs for her, in her present acute stage: more aspirin or other simple salicylates, and cortisone, in substantial amounts. These would help right away.

"Miss Cherry?" Peggy Wilmot said, and Cherry put aside the chart. "I'd like to believe you, but how can I? It hurts every time I move. What will happen to me next?" Her gaze clung to Cherry's. "I thought when my husband died that I knew then what it was to be unhappy—poor Art—"

All in a rush she was telling Cherry about her brief, happy marriage. Her husband had traveled a great deal for the company he worked for. They had moved to Hilton and bought a house here, just a short time before he made his last business trip. As usual, he flew in one of the company's private planes. The plane crashed. Only its burning wreckage was ever found.

Cherry remained silent, pretending she didn't see Peggy trying not to cry.

"That was less than a year ago," Peggy Wilmot said. "Sometimes it feels like ten long years since I've seen Art, and sometimes it seems like yesterday."

Now she was alone. She had her parents, but they lived in California. Her brother, living in Florida and working for a firm that built parts for rockets and missiles, was busy with his work and his own family.

"Well, there's one good, hopeful thing, at least, in all my troubles," Peggy said. "It's surprising—" But instead of going on, she turned her head against the pillow,

as if too tired to talk more. "Miss Cherry," she murmured, "could you have someone bring me the mail
from my house? I'd ask my neighbors, but they're away
on vacation. My mail is in the letter box on the porch,
you don't need a key. Today and every day? It's terribly
important."

Cherry promised. She had no right to ask prying
questions, but she could not help wondering what was
so important in this young woman's mail. She wrote
down Peggy Wilmot's address, then covered her patient
lightly and left the ward.

After a very quick lunch in the hospital cafeteria,
Cherry returned to the classroom. Midge was there;
Cherry gave her Peggy Wilmot's address and asked her
to bring the mail from the porch letter box. Then she
resumed teaching the volunteers.

"I want to stress, class," Cherry said, "that today's
all-day session is preliminary training. Tomorrow you'll
report to wherever you are assigned—Records Room,
Clinic, X-ray, ward duty, whatever—and *there* the
supervisor will give you specific training. But there are
some general things you all must know."

Cherry discussed the hospital setup, emphasizing
how various hospital departments worked together.
She talked very seriously to the class about hospital
ethics. Since all of these young volunteers would come
into contact with patients, Cherry talked about the
psychology of a sick person.

"How do you treat a person in bed?" Cherry said.
"You do *not* talk about his illness to him. Be kind, but

don't be oversympathetic. You're here to get him *out* of the hospital, mentally. Talk to him about the things he *can* do, now; encourage him to feed himself and dress himself. Talk to him about what he will do when he's strong again.

"Don't just let him sit or lie there, keep him active," Cherry said. "Interest him with the book cart, or bring him today's newspaper, or play a game of checkers with him. And when the patient becomes ambulatory, or can get around in a wheelchair, you Jayvees will take several patients outdoors to the hospital garden. Of course you'll be supervised by a nurse. You must never, never take anything upon yourself without orders."

Cherry went on to stress another point.

"You must always say on the phone, 'Such-and-such department or ward, volunteer speaking,'" Cherry said, "juniors must sign in and sign out of the hospital. You absolutely must come when you promised to, and on time."

The class was staring at her so soberly that Cherry smiled and said now they would have a little graduation ceremony. Dr. Fortune and Mrs. Streeter came in to commend the twenty young people, tired by now in the late afternoon. They held a graduation in miniature, but everyone was thinking of tomorrow when they would receive preventive inoculations against infectious diseases and start on-the-job training.

Wednesday morning Cherry reported to Orthopedics at eight. Midge and Dodo were already there, in uniform. Cherry smiled at their freshly scrubbed faces and their eagerness. Midge had a pile of mail for Peggy Wilmot. Cherry said that could wait a few minutes while she introduced the two new ward volunteers around—first to the head nurse, then to Nurse Corsi, the P.N. who took care of convalescents, then to the patients. Liz knew Midge and Dodo slightly from Hilton High School, though they were not in the same class. "Wish I could be a Jayvee," Liz said from her bed. Everyone was glad to see the two young girls in their striped pinafores; their youth was like a tonic for sick people. Miss Julia Greer said:

"I am glad to have you on the ward, Midge and Dorothy, and I know you'll to prove your worth. When you do, then I'll accept you as a part of our nursing team. Come to the nurses' station and you'll see what I mean."

The nurses' station was a desk just outside the ward door; here were a telephone, callboard, bulletin board with the day's orders, various reports. Here the head nurse met daily with her two R.N.'s and the P.N. to give each team member her written assignments for the day. It was important, Miss Greer explained to the two young newcomers, to be aware of the relationship of every team member to each patient. Miss Greer gave no definite assignments to the Jayvees.

Midge and Dodo exchanged a glance that said: "The head nurse doesn't trust us." Cherry cleared her throat rather loudly, and the two girls changed their aggrieved expressions to a professional air.